THE E   DOOR

Escape

Copyright © 2013 by Carla Davis

This is a work of fiction. Names, characters, places, and incidents either are the product of the author's imagination or are used fictitiously, and any resemblance to any persons, living or dead, business establishments, events, or locales is entirely coincidental.

The Escort Next Door

All rights reserved.

This book is protected under the copyright laws of the United States of America. No part of this work may be used, reproduced, or transmitted in any form or by any means, electronic or mechanical, including photocopying, recording and faxing, or by any information storage and retrieval system by anyone but the purchaser for their own personal use.

This book may not be reproduced in any form without the express written permission of Carla Davis except in the case of a reviewer who wishes to quote brief passages for the sake of a review written for inclusions in a magazine, newspaper, or journal—and these cases require written approval from Carla Davis prior to publication. Any reproduction or other unauthorized use of the material or artwork herein is prohibited without the express written permission of the author.

Fonts used with permission from Microsoft

Also by bestselling author

Clara James

~The Escort Next Door Series~

The Escort Next Door

The Escort Next Door: Captivated

The Escort Next Door: Escape

~Her Last Love Affair Series~

Her Last Love Affair

Her Last Love Affair: Breathing Without You

Her Last Love Affair: The Final Journey

Please visit http://amzn.to/15ek5q7

Prologue

Julia Hayes thought she had it all; a husband she adored, three children and a beautiful home. However, she'd begun to sense that there was something wrong in her marriage and soon discovers that the 'something' is the multiple infidelities of her husband. She cannot bring herself to remain in the relationship, but she has a big problem: she agreed to sign a prenup that guarantees she gets almost nothing if the pair separates.

With no college education, she realizes her chances of getting enough money to support herself and three children in a short amount of time is almost impossible. And there's yet another problem, she knows her husband, Paul, will fight her for custody of their kids. She feels that she's backed into an inescapable corner, and that sense of desperation leads her to seek out potential ways of making significant amounts of money in the shortest possible amount of time.

Although it's completely against her nature, she finds herself flirting with the idea of becoming an escort. She's scared by the thought, but she also realizes there's a frisson of excitement to the notion. Having been a 'good girl' all her life, and only ever having slept with the man who ultimately became her husband, the prospect of breaking free from it all is intoxicating.

So she begins to live a double-life: at home she's Julia, the doting wife and devoted mother; while at work she's Arianna, a woman who is whatever her clients want her to be – dominant and aggressive, or quiet and demur, or anything in between, but always irresistibly sexy.

And contrary to her expectations, she loves the job. She enjoys being the center of a man's attention, even if only for one night. She finds it freeing to express herself sexually, and she begins to see some regular clients that she grows very fond of. Of course, the money is also rolling in fast as she gains confidence and her reputation quietly spreads.

Everything seems to be working perfectly. Until the night she meets a particularly aggressive client. The handsome, wealthy man forces her to snort a line of coke before knocking her around the expensive hotel suite and taking her roughly from behind.

The next morning, Julia realizes she's gotten in way over her head and had been naïve about the risks she was taking. Although she hasn't quite saved enough money to fulfill all of her plans, she figures she has enough to put down a deposit on a mortgage and, at least, make a break from her unfaithful husband and loveless marriage.

However, her conviction to get out of the business doesn't last as long as she thought it would. Because a few days later, she receives an email from a man who offers $25,000 to spend an evening with him. She's scared to accept, and bruises from her last job are faint but still present. However, the money is tempting and on instinct alone, she calls the man and agrees to meet him in the lobby of his apartment building.

Julia's client, Preston, is a lawyer who is associated with a homeless children's charity. Together, they attend a dinner and ball to raise money for the charity, and as Julia begins to get to know Preston better, she starts to find herself having a good time. But she's shocked when the night draws to a close and Preston does not invite her into his apartment. Instead, he kisses her goodnight and asks his driver to see her back home.

A mixture of relief and rejection wars within her, until the next morning, when she receives a text message from him – he wants to see her again and is once more willing to offer $25,000 for one night of her time. A part of Julia knows she should decline, take the money she has and get out of this absurd business while she has the chance. However, another part of her is operating on autopilot and has already replied to his message, agreeing to another date.

Chapter One

SECRETARY

Paul had become used to my late night trips to the gym. At least, that was the excuse I gave for my disappearing act. In truth, he probably wouldn't have noticed if I left the house without an explanation at all. In any case, telling Paul that I was going to workout on the Wednesday night Preston had asked me to meet him didn't stir any suspicion in my husband. He wasn't all together happy about it, though.

"So I have to babysit the kids again?" he muttered, sitting on the couch with his feet resting on the coffee table and the New York Times spread out on his lap.

I was in the middle of picking up toys that had been abandoned by our three children and didn't bother to stop. "I don't think it's called babysitting," I told him as I dumped an armful of plastic blocks in the box they were supposed to call home. "I think it's called being a father."

"Yeah, yeah," he said, rolling his eyes but still refusing to lift them from the paper. "The point is, I've got to stay here?"

"You had plans?" I asked. "We could always ask your parents to take them for the night," I suggested.

He was silent for a moment and I wondered if he had indeed had plans. Was he meeting another one of his one-night stands? Was there some young woman at his office that had caught his eye... and other parts of his anatomy? "I...err," he shrugged, "was thinking about having a few beers with some guys from work."

He'd never been one to socialize with the men that worked for him. A year before, I would have said he didn't socialize with the men or women that worked for him, but, of course, I now knew that to be far from the truth. But he certainly wasn't one for making friends with his employees; never had been. Probably because, even when he was junior member of the board, he knew that one day he would take over the company from his father. Back when I thought I knew him, I thought his reserved personality was because he found it awkward to mix business with pleasure; and that he wanted to be respected, so didn't want to be seen in an informal light. With hindsight, I realized it was good old fashioned snobbery. Daddy owned the company, so that made him better than everyone else. It meant he could look down at the men and treat the women as if they were his personal concubines, who existed only to gratify his sexual desires.

The other me, the one who had been oblivious to his affairs, would have brought up the inconsistency of his sudden yearning to buddy up with his colleagues. However, it didn't matter to me any more. Whatever he was really doing, didn't concern me. In fact, if he was going to be meeting a woman, all the better, because if Preston wanted me to stay later than I'd planned, I wouldn't have to worry about Paul getting suspicious. No, my darling husband would be far too busy getting his own kicks.

"Okay," I said, smiling as I bent to pick up a small race car. "I'm sure your mom would be happy to help," I added. "Why don't you give her a call?"

"You're okay with that?" he asked skeptically, sliding his feet down off the glass surface of the coffee table and closing the newspaper.

"The kids staying at your parents?" I asked, my brow creasing. They'd stayed with their grandparents often, especially over the last few months. The children had fun, Paul's folks loved to have them around and Paul's mom, in particular, relished feeling useful.

Of course, she also relished rubbing it in my face, but since the plan to leave had taken root, I was capable of handling it much better. The knowledge that it would only be for a short time longer made it easier to swallow.

"No," he huffed. "Me going out?"

"Why should I mind?" I shrugged.

"No reason, I guess," he muttered, not managing to look at me as he spoke.

I thought, for no more than a second, that I'd seen a glimpse of something that looked like guilt. Did he feel bad about what he'd done; what he was no doubt still doing? After a moment's musing, I dismissed the notion. It didn't matter whether the guilt I thought I saw was there or not, it wouldn't change the way I felt about his betrayal. Besides, I'd done too much and gone too far for things to ever go back to the way they'd been before this whole thing began.

He didn't say anything more. He simply nodded, as he got to his feet and grabbed the cordless phone from the arm of a chair on the opposite side of the room. I heard the beeping of the numbers he punched in as he strolled away, seeking the privacy of his office to make the call.

Part of me wanted to creep up to the door and listen; because I was certain that he was speaking to someone other than his mother. However, I didn't have the opportunity.

"Mom, what are we having for dinner?"

Lizzie's soft voice coming from behind me, made me jump in my skin. "Oh, jeez," I gasped. "You startled me."

"Sorry," she offered, grinning.

Peering down at her, I smiled as I pressed my hand against my pounding heart. "Woo," I puffed, exhaling. "What was it you wanted?" I wondered, realizing I hadn't taken her question in properly.

"What's for dinner?" she repeated, throwing an arm around my waist and hanging on me in a way she hadn't done for a couple of years.

I slipped my arms around her, hugging her close and realizing that my little girl wasn't so little anymore. The top of her head easily reached my chest. My eight-year-old was growing fast and she was turning into a young lady right before my eyes. "I don't know, honey," I soothed, squeezing her tight as though it would stop her inevitable sprint to adulthood. "What do you want?"

"Spaghetti?" she suggested hopefully, her face darting up to mine.

"All right," I nodded, "spaghetti it is."

"Thanks, Mom," she cheered, releasing her hold of me and dashing headlong toward the kitchen. "I love you!" she called, excitedly. She looked a lot like her younger brother as she circled the center island, as giddy as when she was a toddler. It had been a long time since I'd seen her like that. Over recent months, she'd become much more somber and sensible. I'd wondered on more than one occasion if she knew something wasn't right between me and Paul. Looking back, I think she must have sensed it, even if she didn't know exactly what the problem was.

"I love you too, sweetie," I said softly, uncaring whether she even heard me. "There's nothing I wouldn't do for you and your brother and sister," I added in whispered voice. I hoped one day I'd be able to say it and have her understand that I meant it.

Much later that evening, after the kids were all tucked in bed, I returned to the living room to find Paul sitting on the couch. It was unusual for him to sit there, typically if he wanted to watch some TV, he'd do it in his office. That was his sanctuary, his cave; a place that the children never entered and I was only permitted access to bring him food or clean up.

"The other TV not working?" I asked, tipping my head to the small hallway that lead to his den.

"It's fine," he replied, his eyes meeting mine. That in itself was something that had become very rare. "Just thought we could sit together."

"Okay," I nodded, plastering a smile on my face and lowering myself into the seat by his side.

He instantly moved, shuffling along the couch until his hip was pressed against mine. I knew the moment he did so that watching TV was not what he had in mind. Since I'd found out about his affairs and begun my slightly unorthodox career, we hadn't been intimate with each other. On a couple of occasions, he'd tried to instigate something, but predominantly he'd been detached and uninterested in me. Subtly, leaning my face towards his, I inhaled through my nose and quickly realized what was going on. Just like the other times Paul had suddenly found himself feeling amorous toward me, he'd been drinking.

Despite my best attempt to sniff his breath without being noticed, he felt me moving closer and instantly placed his hand on my outer thigh. "Hmm," he hummed, his fingers moving a little higher. "This feels nice."

"Yeah," I lied, swallowing hard. I tried to force myself to relax, with the silent reminder that I acted as though I was interested in men for a living. And yet, I knew that wasn't quite true. I hadn't had to act with most of them – there had been an element of interest in all of them; with the exception of the crazy guy, Scott. None of my other clients had made me feel sleazy or dirty, but being touched by own husband made me feel sick to my stomach. "Umm," I mumbled. "Maybe we shouldn't, though."

"Why not?" he lazily asked, his head drifting to my neck.

"You have to get up early in the morning," I pointed out, placing my own fingers over his to stop their journey upward.

"I don't care," he dismissed; his hand continuing to move upward, disregarding my efforts to stop it. "Do you know how long it's been since we've done it?" he asked, the phrase 'done it' reminding me of our first teenage sexual fumbling's.

"Umm," I replied. "I'm not sure."

"It's been months, baby," he whined.

I knew it hadn't been months since he'd had sex, and his attempt to sound like some poor sex-starved husband wasn't doing anything to endear me to him. "Really?" I asked. "That long?" The truth was I knew exactly how long it had been since we'd last been together. It was four months, three weeks and five days. That's how long it had been since I found the empty condom wrapper in his bag. That was how long it had been since I determined to do whatever was necessary to enable me to get out of this marriage.

His hand had worked its way between my legs and the heel of his palm was pressed tightly against the zipper of my jeans. "I want you," he eagerly said, pushing harder.

The sharp buzz of the telephone caused us both to jump. Paul quickly recovered himself and his hand went back to a very unsexy, rough massaging of my groin. I, however, leaned over the arm of the couch and grabbed the phone that lay on the end table.

"Hello," I greeted, bringing the phone to my ear with one hand while the other grabbed his wrist and tried to yank his fingers away from my body.

"Ohh, errr, hello," came the nervous reply. "Is this Mrs. Hayes?" the woman asked.

"Yes, it is," I replied. "Can I help you?"

"I was wondering if I could talk to your husband," she rapidly said. "My name's Lyra, I'm his new personal assistant."

"Just a sec," I said, before covering the mouthpiece and turning to Paul. "You have a new assistant?" I asked.

"What?" he said, lifting his head.

"Lyra," I explained. "She's on the phone."

His eyes widened and his hand snapped away from me as if he'd been burned. "Oh right," he mumbled, jumping to his feet. "I'll...err, take it in the office." With that, he held out his open palm, waiting for me to place the phone in it.

Clara James

I was left to wonder what had happened between Paul and Lyra, had he made a mistake; gotten involved with a girl who expected more than just sex? Was she threatening to tell me what had happened between them? Did she think she could convince him to leave? If the poor girl had fallen in love with him, I had nothing but sympathy for her. I gladly handed him the phone, watched him jog toward the den before switching off the TV and heading to bed. It was two hours until Paul followed me. By that time, I was faking being asleep and he made no attempt to wake me.

Chapter Two

Evening Romance

Just like our first date, Preston asked me to meet him at his luxury condo. However, this time, he made no requests about wearing a formal gown, so I dressed in a slightly more casual figure-hugging ivory colored dress. Usually when visiting a client, my go-to palette was red or black: the sexy, slutty colors. But Preston had shown himself to be very different from every one of my previous clients and I hoped he'd appreciate a slightly more subtle expression of sexiness. The dress reached my knees, it had a v neck, which wasn't really low enough to show any cleavage, and it had capped sleeves. To sum it up in one word, it was modest. My hair was curled into soft waves and was loose, hanging a little further than my shoulders. My legs were covered in tan colored hold-ups and on my feet were a pair of open-toed, low heels that were silver.

As I walked into the lobby, I was greeted by the familiar smile of the doorman. He was once again sitting behind his desk and this time, had a novel open in front of him. "Hello, Miss," he smiled. "It's nice to see you again."

"Good evening, Hank," I returned the greeting. "I'm here-"

"To see Mr. Verrill," he said for me. "Yes, he mentioned he was expecting you. And, if I might say, he's a very lucky man."

I smiled, dropping my eyes bashfully. Hank didn't seem to notice though, he was already reaching for his phone and calling Preston's home.

"Yes, Sir," he grinned into the handset. "I certainly will." With that he replaced the phone and lifted his face back to mine. "Mr. Verrill asks that you head on up," he said.

"Oh," I replied, slightly taken aback. I'd just assumed that, like last time, he'd meet me in the lobby and we'd head out for our date. "Right," I added, trying to regain my composure.

"It's 403," Hank kindly offered.

"Thanks," I nodded, swiveling on the ball of one foot so I was facing the elevator. I gradually made my way across the pristine floor that shined like a mirror and reached out to push the elevator call button. The doors swished open almost instantly, and I was met by a strong smell of perfume, obviously someone who bathed in Chanel had recently vacated the tiny enclosed space.

I slipped inside, pushed my index finger to the '4' and tried to slow the rapid rhythm of my pulse. Meeting him a second time was possibly more nerve wracking than the first. Although, on the face of it, that made no sense; but it didn't prevent it from being true. I knew that he wasn't a violent man, he'd shown himself to be a perfect gentleman; maybe too much of one. I wasn't concerned for my safety, not my physical safety at least. But there was something else about him, something that seemed to scream 'danger', something that terrified me. Of course the irony was, that same something was what called to me and drew me to accept his proposal for a second date.

His front door was like all the others on the floor, a beautiful redwood with brass numbers screwed to the center. What made Preston's door stand out from the rest was that it had a houseplant in a large terracotta pot to the right of it. It was a strange looking thing; standing around four feet, it was a little like a miniature palm tree, but with wilder, spiky leaves that had red ting on their edges.

Before I had a chance to ring the bell, which was on the opposite side of the door frame, the door itself slowly opened. Preston's head appeared in the gap and he caught me staring at his plant.

"Madagascar dragon tree," he said.

Startled, my eyes snapped up to his. "Oh," I mumbled. "It's...err...very nice," I added, smiling awkwardly.

He grinned broadly, before pulling the door open wider. "Why don't you come on in?" he suggested, making a quick flick with his head in the direction of the apartment.

"Thanks," I politely replied, following his request, side-stepping past him and through the doorway.

He was dressed more casually then the first time I saw him, but he was still very nicely put together with charcoal dress pants, shiny black loafers and a matching leather belt that hugged his slim waist. His shirt was a soft pink with the top button loose. His hair too was in a more free and easy style than I'd seen before. The light brown strands had much less gel in them, giving his style a softer look. A couple of unruly locks had fallen from his side sweep and were resting on his forehead. On this occasion, he wasn't wearing his glasses and I was offered a much better view of his rich, brown eyes.

"It's great to see you again," he said, closing the door.

"You too," I responded, nervously crossing one foot over the other as I stood in the middle of his living room. It was a substantial size, with book shelves lining all of one wall, and windows that opened out onto a large balcony in the other wall. There was hardwood floors beneath my feet, with a square rug that was home to, two three-seater couches placed in an L-shape. In the room were also a coffee table and an entertainment center.

Through an archway to my left, I could see the kitchen. And to my right, there was a hallway; I couldn't see very far down that passageway, but I could see a couple of landscape photographs in frames on the wall.

"Well," he said taking a couple of strides toward me. "I've got dinner coming, do you want to take a seat in here?" he offered. "Or don't you mind seeing the unimpressive wizard behind the curtain?" He smiled, as he gestured to the kitchen with his head.

I laughed at his joke, grateful that he had a knack for breaking the ice. "I...umm..." I paused, figuring out which of the two options was more preferable. Being around him made me terribly anxious, but sitting in the living room with only my thoughts for company would probably work me into an even worse state. "I like to watch a master at work," I eventually concluded.

"Oh, hey, now," he quickly stated, lifting his index finger. "I never claimed to be a master," he corrected me. "Don't go getting your hopes up, I don't want to be the cause of disappointment."

"I'm sure you won't disappoint me at all," I replied innocently and automatically. It only took a beat for the possible subtext to hit me. "Uh, I...errr," I gabbled. "I mean, I-"

"It's okay," Preston grinned. "I know what you mean." Still smiling warmly, he held out his arm encouraging me toward the kitchen. "Come on," he said as I began to move. "I hope you like risotto."

"Yeah," I replied, nodding as I walked past him.

The kitchen was incredibly clean considering he'd been cooking. The counter tops were all dark granite and cupboards were a sleek, modern red color. A pot sat on the stove simmering gently and the scent of asparagus drifted from the grill.

"It's nothing too fancy," he said as he walked up behind me. Placing a hand on my back, he gently turned me to a small dining table, which was set out with plates, silverware and a couple of candles waiting to be lit. "I mean, I like to cook," he added, pulling out a drawer and grabbing a wooden spoon. "But I don't get much time to do it, so I'm certainly no expert." With a self-effacing shrug, he lifted the lid of the pan and gave his rice a brief stir before covering it again. Once he'd taken a quick look at the grill and was satisfied things were coming along nicely, he wandered over to me.

I still stood by the table, one hand resting on the back of a chair, while I tried to think of something to say; it wasn't usually so hard to make conversation with a client. I suspect the problem was that when we went to the charity dinner he'd made such a fuss about getting to know the 'real me'. I was more than a little reluctant, to say the least, and it had made me clam up.

"Wine?" he asked, pointing to a bottle of red that was already on the table.

"Please," I nodded.

Before I'd replied, he was already opening the bottle. He poured me a glass before pouring one for himself. Offering me my drink, he picked up his own and lifted it. "To..." he began, his eyes searching the ceiling. "A great evening?" he suggested.

"To a great evening," I echoed softly, clinking my glass to his. I was careful to sip slowly on the wine and was even more careful not to consume too much over dinner. Although it would have done wonders for my nerves, I was worried about what I might do, or more importantely, say while under the influence. Ironically, Preston had something about him that made it easy to be myself; made me *want* (on some level at least) to be myself. I had to keep a lid on that unruly side.

Once the meal was served, I was able to chat about the food and then, eventually, found my way onto the topic of his work. "Have you been busy?" I wondered aloud, feeling that even though he was previously reluctant to talk about his career, the workload itself was something we could dwell on for a few minutes.

"Hmm," he hummed, chewing his mouthful and swallowing before saying anything more. "Umm, yeah, I guess so," he nodded, reaching for his wine and washing the remnants of food down with it. "Actually, one of my colleagues keeps asking about you," he added.

"Excuse me?" I replied, sure I must have misheard him.

He nodded slowly, as he chuckled. "Yeah, his name's Ralph. I don't think you ever met him at the ball, but he saw me with you and he's been badgering me."

"Oh," I replied, for want of anything else to say. I'd never had a client named Ralph, but perhaps he'd given me another name. Was it possible that Preston had heard the details of what I'd done with another man? "He knows me?" I asked, my brow creasing in anxiety more than curiosity.

"No," he said, his eyes widening slightly. "No, I don't think so. He just thinks you're beautiful and wants to know how I came to meet a woman like you."

"Oh," I repeated, this time with a deflated tone. I was glad that Ralph wasn't a client, or should I say former client, but the facts surrounding Preston's meeting me was not something I was thrilled to have shared with his colleagues. "I'm sure his opinion of me changed when you told him."

"Told him what?" Preston asked, genuine confusion etched in his expression.

With a scoff of self-derision, I shook my head. "You know what, I'm sorry," I whispered, reaching for my glass and tipping a large mouthful straight down my throat. "I'm not being very good company," I added. "Let's talk about something else."

"No, I want to know what you meant," he insisted, his features still studying me closely.

Using the index finger of my left hand to sweep some hair from my right shoulder, I replaced the glass on the table. I hesitated, before finally shrugging and trying to dismiss the subject. "It's nothing," I assured him calmly.

"It's something to me," he countered. "I'm serious, I want to know what you think I told him."

"I don't know," I huffed. "The truth?"

"Which is?" he prompted, fixing me with a serious, almost overbearing stare.

"That I'm just a whore you picked up," I answered, unashamedly maintaining eye contact.

Preston's jaw dropped fractionally open, but he said nothing for a few seconds. Instead, he leaned back in his seat, his head tipped to one side and he tapped his upper teeth thoughtfully with his tongue. "You believe that's what I think of you?" he eventually uttered, his words quiet.

My eyes moved over his face, and I thought I saw what looked like hurt in it. However, I quickly dismissed that from my mind; why on Earth would he be hurt by my assumption about his perception of me? Nevertheless, his expression continued to render me mute.

Suddenly, and with a scrape of chair legs, he got to his feet. He quickly made his way around the small table and gripped my hand, which sat limply on the table. It wasn't hard enough to hurt me, but it was more than enough for me to realize that I'd upset him. Without a word, he tugged on my wrist, coaxing me to my feet. I obeyed without a fight and as soon as

I was standing, he placed his other hand on my waist, turning me to face him.

"Is that how you think I see you?" he asked, refusing to release my hand.

"I..." I mumbled. "I...I don't know."

"Is that how you see yourself?" he continued.

I could no longer look at him. My eyes darted over his shoulder, fixing on the oven and the pot that still sat upon the stove.

"Hey," he urged, the fingers that had been clasping my wrist moving to my face. With a feather light brush, the backs of his fingers caressed my cheekbone. "Is that what you think?" he repeated, his brow crinkling in concern and his eyes boring into me as if he wanted to get all the way to my soul.

"I don't know," I blurted, my voice suddenly tearful. The lump in my throat rose and the stinging began at the backs of my eyes. "I don't know any more," I added, a single droplet escaping onto my cheek. "I thought I was in control, that I knew what I was doing...But it's all...I don't know anything anymore." The words came in a jerky, emotional mess that didn't even make much sense to me.

Preston's response was both confusing and unexpected. As the fingers that had stroked my cheek moved into my hair, he gently grasped the back of my head and pulled me toward him. Without a word, he melded his soft lips to mine.

Chapter Three

HOW DO YOU KNOW

Preston kept a tender but tight hold of my hand as he led me into his bedroom. By then, my tears had dried in almost invisible, salty streaks. My heart was fluttering in my chest and, although I was no more capable of rational speech, it was for a very different reason.

He'd said nothing as he'd tentatively explored my lips with several more soft kisses. No words had been uttered before those explorations had turned more frenzied and his tongue quested entrance into my mouth. Speech hadn't seemed necessary as the hand at my waist moved to entwine with my fingers and we wandered from the kitchen.

This man was no less of a mystery to me. In fact, if anything, he was more of one. There I'd been, an emotional wreck, and he still seemed interested in taking me to bed. Was he that desperate? No, there was more to it than just sex – even then, in my muddle-headed state, I think I realized that. For reasons unknown to me, and perhaps unknown to both of us, he appeared to be drawn to me in a similar way I'd experienced with him. Maybe his better judgment was telling him to kick the crazy bitch out of his apartment while he still could, but if that was the case, another part of him was fighting it.

Gently, with his free hand, he grasped the circular doorknob of his room and opened it. As he pushed it wide, he glanced over his shoulder at me. I don't know what he saw in my face, but whatever it was caused him to flash a reassuring smile, before crossing the threshold and pulling me softly behind him.

He didn't stop moving until he'd reached a step or two from the foot of his bed. When his feet did come to a stop, he turned to face me. "Do you want to know what I think of you?" he asked, a soft half smile lightening the seriousness of his face.

Moistening my lips with the tip of my tongue, I looked questioningly back at him, but he didn't elaborate. "I...I..." I stammered.

"Well, I'm going to show you," he stated, his fingers slowly disengaging from mine. Both hands lifting, he placed them comfortingly on my shoulders, while his thumbs stroked the bare flesh at my clavicles.

What was about to happen struck me like a ton of bricks. He'd paid a ridiculous amount of money for this and I was in no state to dazzle him. But money aside, I was desperate not to disappoint this man. "Preston," I whispered. "Maybe I should go," I suggested weakly. "I can come back another night, when I'm not such a mess and...err..."

He hushed any further effort to speak by molding his mouth to mine in a slow steady lean forward. When he began to pull away his lower lip clung to mine a little longer than the rest of him. "I don't want you to leave," he softly explained.

"But...I," I insisted, shaking my head. I tried to take a step back, but he kept his hands on my shoulders and his feet moved in sync with mine, keeping us exactly as close as we had been. "I'm not....Your paying me a lot of money and-"

Again, he silenced me with a kiss; this time trailing the very tip of his tongue between my slightly parted lips. Gradually he slid it from left to right, prompting me to whimper helpless against his mouth.

29

I don't know whether he was just trying to shut me up or if he realized he could render me incapable of thinking the anxious, tense thoughts that were bombarding my brain. In fact, he could render me incapable of thinking much of anything at all. I was quickly heading that way. Concerns about the businesslike nature of what brought us to that moment, were beginning to recede. The worry that I had what was a totaled $50,000 obligation to fulfill, disappeared like a faint scent in the breeze. The only thing that filled my mind was the feel of his hands, his lips, his tongue, the taste of him, the smell of him and the heat of his body so close to my own.

Preston's hands were running down my arms and reaching around my back, while his tongue extended a little further from the confines of his own mouth. It swirled and entwined with mine, like two vines so tangled and connected that it's difficult to tell where one ends and the other begins. As he tipped his head to the right, slanting his lips over mine and tasting the roof of my mouth, his breath came soft against my cheek. It was the most seemingly insignificant sensation, but it caused goose bumps to break out all over the back of my neck. My own hands, which had up until then been uselessly hanging by my sides, sprang into action curling around his waist and grasping the smooth shirt at his back.

So transfixed by that gently brush of air against my face, I didn't realize his fingers had reached the zipper of my dress and he was beginning to pull it down. Nothing about his movements was rushed, clumsy or frantic. It was as if he'd carefully choreographed every action. As he used his right hand to glide the zipper down to the small of my back, his left hand followed; the tips of his fingers caressing every inch of my skin that was exposed. It was such a delicate brush that it was almost ticklish.

I gave a muffled groan of protest, as he disconnected his mouth from mine. Quickly opening my eyes, I found him peering down at me with a radiant smile. His fingers meanwhile had once again found my shoulders and were confidently pushing down the fabric of my dress. As it reached my upper arms, gravity took over and the dress puddled at my abdomen. His hands were almost instantly at my hips, helping it the rest of the way. When it hit the floor, I watched his face closely. His gaze moved down my legs, lingering at the top of the tan holdups, before his eyes slowly made a return journey, seeming to caress me as they moved over my hips, my belly and the cleavage that was pushed up by a white, lace Wonderbra. Finally, and with an even broader grin, his focus returned to my face.

Expecting him to immediately begin removing my underwear, he surprised me when, instead, he resumed the kiss that had been driving me crazy. It was a little more intense though, his tongue coaxing mine into a playful wrestle that moved smoothly from my mouth to his and back again. As my toes started to curl, and my hips begin to move involuntarily against him, my right hand twisted in the cotton of his shirt and gripped him ever more tightly.

One of his hands was at my hip and could no doubt feel the gently undulating motion that had overwhelmed any conscious ability to prevent it. But again, he did the unexpected, rather than pulling me more firmly to him and grinding against me, his fingers continued their exquisitely tender stroking. He traced the top of my panties before softly making his way down the seam and trailing the arch of the elastic which clung to the top of my leg. As he bought his hand around the back and the curve of my bottom, he slipped the tip of his index finger beneath the fabric and scorched the flesh with a liquid fire.

I'd never known a sensation quite like that; never realized a touch that was so barely there could be felt so powerfully. With a low, rumbling moan of pleasure, my hips instantly bucked and my mound bumped the hot, throbbing swell of his groin.

"Hmm," he chuckled, pulling away from my mouth. "Sorry," he whispered, "didn't mean to startle you."

I didn't contradict him. It wasn't that I didn't want to, but I was embarrassed to admit that the slightest touch of his finger on a tiny piece of skin at the edge of my bottom had turned me on as much as it had.

He didn't seem perturbed though, and as both hands began to work their way up my back, he gripped the clasp of my bra. My breath and pulse were racing as heat flushed my cheeks, flooded my solar plexus and crept into the crotch of my underwear. He freed my breasts, guiding the straps down my arms and allowing the bra to drop to the floor beside my dress.

For several seconds, he didn't touch me, didn't move nor did he speak. Then, gradually, he dipped his head. Again, he surprised me by ignoring the obvious. Rather than honing in on a nipple, he gently caressed the side of his face across the front of one breast and pressed his lips to the outer edge, just beneath my armpit. His mouth continued to draw an invisible path of kisses down the curve and eventually beneath my breast, before coming back up the valley between them. He treated the opposite sphere of smooth, tender white flesh to the same treatment before cupping the weight of both breasts in his warm, sure hands. It was only then that he brought his face to one nipple. He began by teasing it lightly with his tongue, light flicks that stiffened it to an even more rigid peak.

Listlessly, my head flopped back and my hand swept up to the back of his neck, rubbing in leisurely circles at the edge of his hairline. As the warmth and wetness of his mouth enveloped my tight bud and he began to suck enthusiastically, I inhaled a shaky breath. "Oh, God," I whimpered.

I lost myself to that feeling for quite some time, exactly how long I'm unsure. I know that Preston took his time over both breasts, massaging them with soothing, soft hands and simultaneously sucking, licking and kissing with an eager mouth that set me aflame with restlessness. And at some point, the realization that I'd been passively accepting a lot of pleasure, but offering very little in return, kicked in.

As he continued to memorize my bosom with his fingers, lips and tongue, I continued to gently stroke the nape of his neck. My free hand meanwhile drifted down his torso, over his hip and around to his backside. I found his butt rounded and deliciously firm. I grasped it firmly, causing him to groan against the inner curve of my right breast. Pleased with his reaction, I curled my fingers back round to the front. Slipping my hand over his groin, I stroked gently up and down the firm ridge I found. Then, I carefully placed a finger beneath the fabric of his fly and grasped the zipper.

Feeling this, Preston's head shot up. "Not yet," he softly said, his hand covering mine and gently pulling it away. "Not yet," he repeated, smiling now as he continued to grip my fingers and brought them up to his face. With heavy-lidded eyes, he glanced down at my hand, before dropping his mouth to it and pressing his lips to each of the four knuckles.

More than a little shell-shocked, I must have been looking quizzically at him. But he didn't let that distract him. When he'd finished kissing the back of my hand, he turned it over and stroked his bottom lip against the inside of my wrist. My eyes instantly closed shut and I exhaled breathlessly. I felt him smile against my skin, before finding my pulse with the tip of his tongue. At the time, I was in a haze of pleasure and anticipation; and wasn't able to figure out how he seemed to know exactly where and how to touch me. All I knew was that his body was familiar with mine in a way I couldn't understand. It was almost as if we'd made love countless times before. And yet, the experience maintained the excitement and thrill of being brand new for both of us.

Eventually, he released my hand and began to unbutton his own shirt. When I noted what he was doing, I tried to help, but my hands were trembling violently and I didn't manage much more than pushing the cotton from his shoulders. When my eyes met the expanse of chest before me, I sucked in a breath that refused to be expelled again. He was beautiful. I'm sure he would prefer a more masculine description, but there really is no other word for it.

I'd realized he was in shape and trim, but those shirts concealed something I could never have imagined lay beneath the straitlaced exterior I'd seen up until then. The muscles of his shoulders were strong and defined, leading to smooth, hard planes of pecs. Below that, his abdomen contained six beautifully sculptured ab muscles. Nowhere on his belly or his hips was there an ounce of spare flesh; everywhere was sleek, taut skin. Unable to resist its call, my fingers carefully examined his body; my fingertips tracing every line of hard muscle.

He, meanwhile, was looping both arms around my waist and tugging me close. With our bodies pressed together, I wiggled my hips over his groin and stifled a moan as my breasts met his hard chest; hot skin on hot skin. My hands were caught between our joined abdomens and I moved them around his oblique's. He chuckled and squirmed slightly under my light touch and I realized he was ticklish. For some reason, that made him even more attractive in my eyes and I found myself grinning broadly up at him.

"Hey," he attempted to grumble, but his smile gave the game away; he wasn't really disgruntled.

"Hey," I echoed in a lighter tone.

For a second, he looked like he wanted to say something more. But he remained quiet, keeping his hold of my waist as he slowly sank down to his knees.

Chapter Four

SEEDS OF DESIRE

With his head level with my panties, I was suddenly uncomfortable. He would no doubt be able to smell the musky scent of my arousal and he was very close to feeling just how wet the crotch of my underwear was. However, as I tried to step back, he continued to hold me at my waist.

"I want you right here," he softly said, before kissing my abdomen. "Trust me," he added, his words muffled with his lips still attached to my skin.

Once I'd stopped my feeble attempt to move away from him, his hands slid over my hips and eventually down to my legs. He focused first on the right leg, taking the top of the hold-up and slowly rolling it down. When it reached my ankle, he lifted my foot, removed my shoe and tossed the nylon onto the floor. He repeated the slow sensual act with my left leg. He then kept my leg in his hand once he'd stripped it of clothing. In fact, he eased it a touch higher, eventually placing the back of my knee over his shoulder.

I could do nothing but stare down at him, feeling a little unsteady on the one foot that was still on the ground. The top of his head turned to my inner thigh that was now close to his cheek, he then began to trail open-mouthed kisses upward. My breath caught noisily in the back of my throat with every tease of his lips and quick lap of his tongue. Inching higher and higher, until he reached the edge of my panties.

By that point, he must have known just how aroused I was. My drenched underwear was no more than an inch from his face. However, no smart remark; no cocky, gloating comment came from him. Instead, he simply hooked his two index fingers on either side of the white lace and began to ease the panties from my hips.

Just like the hold-ups, he disrobed me slowly, seeming as though he had all the time in the world and wanted to savor every second of it. And when I was finally completely naked before him, he continued to take his time. Now, tossing my right leg over his shoulder and treating it to the same delightful trail of his mouth.

"Oh, God," I gasped, when his lips were just a breath away from my sex. He still wasn't quite touching that place that was so desperate for him, but he was close enough to make me wonder if it was possible to die from sexual anticipation. With trembling hands, I cupped either side of his head, and simply held it, ignoring the urge to direct him. God knows, he didn't need me to; he knew exactly where he was going and how he wanted to get there.

When the heat of his tongue finally ventured between my slick folds, I held back a screech of joy, my eyes clamping shut so I could focus on nothing but the feeling of him. As he slowly lapped up to my clitoris, he hummed slowly and when he hit that swollen bud of nerve endings, I unconsciously bucked as if I'd been slapped on the behind.

I was sure I could feel him chuckle against me, but he didn't pull back and didn't remove the pressure of his mouth. He seemed to sense how sensitive I was; how close; how much I needed the sensation of release. Preston's tongue began a game of tag with my clit, swirling over it or tapping it; his movements gradually increasing in pressure, but always maintaining control.

Control was something I was quickly losing. My hands were moving in hurried circles, mimicking the motion of his tongue and messing his hair in the process. As he edged me higher and higher to the peak, I felt the back of my legs quaking. It was causing my whole body to shake and I felt sure I was about to fall.

While my breath started to come in heavy and strangled pants, my head flopped back. With my face turned to the ceiling, I felt Preston's hands move over my buttocks and up to the small of my back. He tugged me closer to him, as he moaned gently against my body.

That sound and the vibration it caused was enough to send me into a whimpering, breathless mess. "Ugh," I moaned. "God, I...Preston!" White flashes of light sparked in front of my eyelids and the trembling of my legs became violent in their intensity. My whole body constricted and my hands still feverishly stroked through his gorgeous, soft hair.

When the sound of my own heartbeat began to give way to other noises and an awareness of the world began to return, I gradually opened my eyes. Peering down, I found Preston's head still pressed to my groin, only not as intensely as before. Now he was tenderly kissing my outer sex, making his way out to the crease of my leg, then the other, and finally up to my mound. By the time he'd finished this journey, I was soothed, temporarily satisfied and possessed a burning desire to treat him to an equally intimate experience. So, as he began to straighten, I began to sink to my own knees.

He gave me an amused quirk of an eyebrow, as I hungrily pressed my lips to his as our faces passed one another. It was brief, but I hoped it communicated the depth of my gratitude for the way he'd so tenderly worked his magic. If not, perhaps what I had up my own sleeve would demonstrate it beyond a doubt.

I tried to undress him as slowly as he had me, knowing what that luxurious experience had done for my arousal; but my fingers were nowhere near as controlled as his were and I fumbled quickly with his belt. Once his pants were unfastened, I gripped the fabric at his knees and yanked them down to his ankles. Keeping my eyes on him, I slid an index finger into the thick waistband of his boxers and ran it teasingly from left to right, stretching the material just slightly.

He swallowed, as he appeared to have difficulty regulating his breathing. The tent at the front of his shorts was significant and I imagined he was getting very uncomfortable in there. However, I ratcheted up the tension just a notch more, trailing my tongue over the arch of his hipbone, before finally tugging his underwear done to meet his pants.

"Ugh," he groaned in relief, his shaft springing free from the black cotton boxers.

As it did, my fingers stilled. He was huge, bigger than any other man I'd been with. He was wonderfully thick, too. Veins standing proudly, just waiting to be licked. His shaft was rigid with a slight upward curve; and the soft, domed head was sleek and beckoning. It, like his chest, was a vision to behold. Framed at his pubic bone by neat curls of almost jet black hair and joined at the base by his tender, pulsing twin sacks. He smelled clean, but with the faint odor of masculine sweat and musk.

More than a little worried about how well I'd be able to perform given his size, I tentatively began by lapping at the very tip of him, finding it damp. He shuddered at my touch and I felt emboldened. Taking my tongue on a clockwise trip, I circled his head then switched direction. I continued to do this a couple more times, hearing him rumble deep in his chest, I took that as a sign he was enjoying it. Then, I became braver and carefully wrapped my lips around his glans. With one hand, I grasped the shaft and with the other I cupped his balls, rolling them gently in the palm of my hand.

"Ugh," he grunted, his hips jerking very slightly. His hands meanwhile had found the sides of my face. However, he wasn't instructing me with them, nor was he holding me in order to thrust. He simply held me loosely, his thumbs occasionally stroking my cheekbones.

After sucking on his baby soft skin for a few seconds, I tipped back, took a breath and looked up into his face. His expression was one of almost wonderment, and I remember being confused by that. Surely, he'd experienced much better than my feeble attempt at fellatio – I may have been more experienced than when I began escorting, but I was still no expert.

Dismissing the thoughts, I turned my attention back to his erection and this time, as I took his head into my warm mouth, I twisted the hand that held his shaft.

"Arianna," he mumbled in a half-gasp.

I did it again, moving my wrist in a twisting action and this time stroking my way up as my mouth sucked and my tongue swirled.

"Oh, shit," he panted. "Wait," he added, the hands at my face suddenly tightening their grip slightly. "Wait, wait."

Keeping my hands on him, I carefully removed my mouth, peering up at him in question.

His breath coming hard, he appeared as though he'd just completely a 100 meter sprint. "I...umm..." he managed to say between rapid inhales. "I don't want this to be over just yet," he eventually added.

Before I could ask a question, he was bending at the knees and scooping me up. Once he got me in standing position and my fingers had dropped away from his manhood, he smiled warmly. Then turning me, he backed me gradually toward the bed.

I allowed him to lead me back and lay me down on the soft mattress. Instinctively, I was already parting my legs, but he didn't immediately slip between them. Instead, he nestled by my side. Leaning on one hand, he used the other to smooth over my abdomen, while his mouth attached once more to my breast.

I tried to touch him, but it wasn't easy in my position. All I could really do was stroke the arm that was at my waist and clutch at the back of his head.

Soon, however, his hand was moving, working its way lower, gently making its way over my mound, before fingers began to slip between my dampness. He circled my clitoris, which was almost still as sensitive as it had been under the attention of his mouth. Then, the pads of two fingers began to move lower and I arched my back, tilting my entrance to him in welcome.

It was only his index finger to begin with, slowly sliding into my wetness, gradually working its way deeper as it stroked my channel. Then, eventually, he introduced a second finger and carefully moved both in a circular motion, stretching me; preparing me for something larger. My hips were still tipped up to him and his actions were accompanied by my soft sobs of pleasure.

All the time, he continued to taste my breasts, moving from one to the other, always finding new places to tease and never neglecting even an inch of skin. By the time he moved to my sternum, then up to my throat and then the underside of my chin, his fingers were slowly stroking in and out in a rhythm as old as time itself. It felt good, it felt really good. But I needed something more – and I was desperate to give him something too.

"Please," I choked out, my voice barely recognizable even to my own ears. "Please, Preston."

He didn't make me beg. He was already moving, kicking off his pants, shoes and boxers. Eventually, his fingers left me and he quickly disposed of his socks, too. Then, gracefully, he rolled on top of me, his thick erection trapped against my inner thigh and most of his weight braced on the hands he placed right next to my shoulders.

My own hands stroked up his forearms, eventually gripping his biceps as best I could. Lifting my head, I nibbled at his neck and shoulder, mumbling nonsense words of encouragement, as I waited for him to make us one.

Clara James

He shifted his hips with ease and his bulbous glans seemed to find my willing entrance without any assistance, from his hands or mine. However, he didn't rush this last step. Just as he had with everything until that moment, he took his time and exercised incredible control.

He moved slickly with our combined arousal, but he was still careful as he slowly dipped just the tip, back and forth, going a touch deeper each time, feeling me softly yielding to him. "Hmm," he moaned, taking my left earlobe into his mouth and sucking seductively.

I bucked my hips, trying to edge him further. I whimpered as he delved in another inch. I was completely open to him, I knew that I could now take him all the way. And I guess he must have sensed it too, because he suddenly pushed his hips to mine and buried himself to the hilt. We both cried out, his a grunt of intensity and mine a squeal of delight. I'd never known a feeling quite like it, so deliciously full; so complete, so right.

We remained that way for a while, his mouth covering mine. Sharing noisy, wet, passionate kisses, we both relished the sensation of being one. But soon, I began to get restless, I needed to feel him moving inside me and my hips began to jerk beneath him.

He heeded that silent cry, lifting his upper body so he could brace his thrusts on his arms. He stared intently at me, as he gradually eased back, watching the changing expressions as I experienced each sensation intensely. I felt the tiny ridges of his manhood stroking my G-spot before almost disappearing into me entirely. However, with a perpetual motion, it returned just as it had left.

I wrapped my legs tightly around him, inching them higher in a bid to feel him even deeper still. Again, he knew what I wanted and how best to achieve it. One hand swiftly left the bed and hooked under my left knee. He coaxed it higher and higher until I could rest it on his shoulder. By then, I felt certain he was as deep in me as was possible. I felt him bump my cervix, which was a delightful mixture of pleasure and pain. "Argh, God," I whispered.

"You Okay?" he softly asked, his voice as soothing as a warm bath.

"Yes," I panted, before turning my face to the right and biting his forearm. I didn't sink my teeth in hard, but the urge to take hold of something was irresistible.

His response was another thrust, a little faster this time. "Jesus," he muttered.

"Ohh," I exhaled, the mixture of his pelvic bone grinding against my clit and the rubbing of my G-spot, made it impossible to have an awareness of anything else. "Again," I panted.

I don't think he needed my direction. However, he pulled back and returned to me with an enthusiasm that knocked the wind out of me. He was beginning to find a rhythm now; one that was working us both up into a sweaty, breathless frenzy. Over and over again, he plunged into my body, stoking the fire in my belly every time.

And then I came. Completely unexpectedly, from nowhere, the explosion came. A frenzy of sensation that was almost too much to bear. I opened my mouth, tried to cry out my pleasure, but no sound emerged. In fact, no breath was exhaled from my lungs; they'd ceased to function properly. As the waves continued to crash, my body convulsed beneath him, twitching and jerking as thousands of sparks of electricity rocked from my core to every extremity. Then, after what felt like an eternity in that moment, I was once again able to suck in a hurried breath.

I was panting even harder than before, and became aware of the fact that Preston had stopped his rhythmic thrust.

"You okay?" he asked, his cheeks flushed, beads of sweat clinging to his forehead and his eyes dark with desire.

"Yeah," I weakly nodded. "Don't stop," I urged.

He kissed me deeply, before resuming the motion of his lower half. It didn't take more than another three drives of his hips for his entire body to stiffen. "God," he whispered. "Oh, yes!" he grunted, as his seed was rapidly expelled from his body. It wasn't until that moment that I suddenly remembered neither of us had thought to stop for protection. His warmth was pulsing into me and, as it did, my own body responded with another orgasm that caused my sex to squeeze him tightly; coaxing yet more of his essence from him.

Chapter Five

MORNING

As we lay still, most of his weight still taken on his arms, but a reassuring bulk keeping me pinned to the bed, we both listened as our combined breathing began to steady and slow. His head was nestled in the crook of my shoulder, his lips slowly kissing my neck.

My exhausted leg slipped off his shoulder and landed on the mattress, while my hands stroked over his damp, clammy back; moving in lazy patterns. "Wow," I whispered toward the ceiling.

I felt him smile, as his mouth moved down my throat and shoulder. "I'm sorry," he said, eventually finding the strength to lift his head. "I should have....I meant to," he stumbled, his brain still fogged. "I meant to put a condom on, but I guess I just got carried away and..."

"It's okay," I replied. "I got carried away, too." Suddenly concerned about what conclusions he might draw, I quickly qualified that. "It's never happened before. I'm always really careful."

"It's all right," he chuckled, silencing me by pressing his lips to mine. A satisfied rumbling hum vibrated low in his chest, as he pulled away from the kiss. "You know," he sighed gently settling onto his side and rolling us both until our positions were reversed and I was on top of him. Throughout the smooth motion, he remained within me, softening, but not quite completely flaccid. "I've never made love to a woman and not known her name."

"Huh?" I asked, setting my knees on the mattress and placing my hands on his chest to push myself upright.

"It's okay," he smiled. "If you don't want to tell me, I understand. But..." he breathed, his eyes wearily and blissfully moving over my face. "I really would love to know."

"You do know my name," I insisted quietly.

"Well," he nodded as best as he could with the back of his head pressed into the pillow, "I know you sometimes call yourself Arianna." As he spoke, the hands that were loosely splayed on my hips moved reverently up my torso, up to my shoulders where he pushed my hair back and eventually cradled both sides of my face. "But that's not the real you, is it?"

"I...I..." I nervously babbled, feeling like a bug under a microscope. Why did I always feel like he was studying me; trying to penetrate the surface? Of course, I knew what he'd find beneath would disappoint him.

"It's okay," he repeated. "I'm not going to make you tell me."

Trying to relax, I forced a smile that probably looked pained.

"There is one thing I do want to know, though," he added. "Do you have to go?"

"Excuse me?"

"I'd like you to stay, if you can," he explained, the fingers of his right hand tracing the shell of my ear, while the other moved down my neck and traced the dip between my collarbones. "If you don't want to, or if you have somewhere you need to be-" he said, shrugging.

"No," I interjected quickly. "No, I don't have to leave."

"Good," he replied, grinning from ear to ear, as he pulled me down to him.

I didn't have to fake my enthusiasm for staying with him. I've never been more glad of anything in my life than I was about the fact Paul wouldn't be home to expect me back. And while Preston was more preoccupied with exploring my body than he was with getting to know the 'real me', being in his company was one of the best experiences I'd known.

Our second coupling, not that we ever disconnected from the first, was a much lazier affair. I remained on top of him, but didn't have the strength to pump myself up and down his length. So I simply moved my hips back and forth. The climax was slow in the making, and when it came, it wasn't with the explosive blinding power of its predecessors. But it was a sweet sensation, like the expanding ripples on an otherwise calm stretch of water. It caused my eyes to roll back in my head with delight.

After that, he continued to caress and kiss me until eventually, in a tangled mess of arms and legs, we fell into a deep and very contented slumber. And, for a few hours at least, I was truly happier than I'd been in a very long time.

But the morning brought with it a big dose of awkward. After showering, dressing and brushing my teeth with some toothpaste on my finger, I just wanted to get out of there. For one thing, I was expected to pick up the kids from the in-laws and for another, I felt incredibly vulnerable. Despite my best efforts to keep him at arm's length, I realized that it had been a waste of time. I might not have told him my name or anything about myself, but I'd shown him the real me – I'd made love to him as myself. I hadn't been Arianna, and I think we both knew it.

"You're welcome to stay for breakfast," he insisted, running a hand through his sleep-tussled hair, before fastening the belt of his robe. "I can whip something up or there's some cereal," he suggested hopefully.

"I really have to go," I replied, slipping into my shoes and checking the floor to make sure I hadn't left anything at the foot of his bed.

"Okay," he nodded, trying to sound blasé, but failing miserably. "Well, I'll just get my checkbook," he said, already moving toward an antique, oak roll top desk.

"No," I blurted, stopping his movements as he reached for a drawer on the left of the desk. "I...umm...I can't accept that," I mumbled.

"Why not?" he asked, confusion crinkling his brow. Without waiting for an answer, he pulled the drawer open and grasped for something inside.

"I mean it," I urged. "I really can't take that from you."

It was his glasses he held between his finger and thumb. He unfolded the arms and slipped the frames onto his face, before continuing his line of questioning. "I don't understand, I thought we had an agreement?"

"Yeah," I responded, nodding halfheartedly. "But last night..." I began, stopping when I found the words sticking in my throat. Pushing a few damp strands of hair behind my ear, I took a deep breath, before forging ahead once more. "Last night was much more than an 'agreement', it was more than business, to me at least, and I can't take that money from you."

Finally understanding, he smiled. Moving away from the desk, he padded barefoot to the bed and sat on the edge of it, facing me. "It was much more than business to me," he softly announced. "But I want to help you."

Eyeing him warily, I was more than a little reticent about asking him to explain. "What do you mean?" I muttered.

He was just as pensive in his answer. "I don't know what kind of trouble you are in," he slowly said, keeping his eyes earnestly fixed on mine. "But you obviously need this money for something and whatever it is, I want to help."

My defenses flying up, I scoffed almost derisively. "What makes you think I'm in trouble?"

Unflappable, Preston continued to watch me with a calm expression of openness. "I don't think you'd be doing this unless you'd found yourself in a jam."

"You know, for someone who doesn't even know my name, you profess to know an awful lot about me," I blurted. What had gotten under my skin more than his accurate words was the way he looked at me; those eyes that swept into my being without permission. They frightened me.

"I'm not trying to upset you," he reasoned, his arms resting on his thighs and his hands loosely entwined between his slightly parted legs. "I just want to help, if I can."

"Yeah," I whispered. "Well, I don't need you to rescue me. I'm going to be just fine." With that, I quickly bolted to the door. I could hear him following me, but he made no attempt to stop me and said nothing as I practically ran down the hallway. I grabbed my purse from where I'd left it on the couch, and then lunged for the front door. However, when I got there, the damn thing wouldn't open. I tugged, I twisted what looked like the lock, but I couldn't get it to budge.

Calmly, Preston's arm reached over my shoulder twisted the lock in the opposite direction and held it there while his other hand turned the handle. "I'm sorry," he said, as he tugged the door open wide. "I didn't mean to offend you."

I peered at the clear doorway, then back at him not trying to prevent me from leaving, but offering his simple and heartfelt apology. Not that he needed to say it. "I know," I mumbled. "I know you didn't. I'm sorry for getting upset."

"So, can we talk?" he suggested.

"No," I replied, shaking my head firmly. "I really do have to go."

"Okay," he smiled, with an accepting nod. "Can I see you again?" he added.

Swallowing, I warred with the part of me that wanted to throw myself into his arms right then and there. "I don't think that's a very good idea," I breathed, unsure whether any sound had actually come out of my mouth. I shook my head apologetically, opening my mouth to say something else. But unable to find my voice, I quickly turned to the door and hurried across the threshold. I didn't look back as my feet rapidly moved down the corridor toward the elevator.

When I got to the lobby, I was glad to see that Hank's shift was over and he'd been replaced by another security guard; a younger man, who acknowledged me with a nod.

60

It was after eight when I got home, and another moment of relief came when I learned that Paul wasn't there yet. He must have made quite a night of it, too. However, the thought of what he might have been doing the same time I was with Preston was tainting my memory of the night before, so I quickly shook those musings from my brain. It didn't matter; none of it mattered any more. I had enough money to get away from him, so the charade had to end.

I quickly chucked my clothes, putting on some jeans and a sweater before leaving the house once more and heading to Paul's parents. His mother complained that I was thirty minutes late and pointed out that I wasn't wearing any make-up and looked like I hadn't got a wink of sleep. Apologizing for my tardiness and what was, apparently, an unacceptably disheveled appearance, I explained that I'd got back late from the gym and had trouble unwinding. I'm not sure if she believed me. The suspicious way she eyed my entire figure suggested she did not.

"Well, maybe you're spending too much time at this gym," she shrilly announced.

"Yeah," I shrugged. "Maybe."

"Maybe you should be spending more time with your family," she continued. "I'm sure Paul's not happy about all the evenings you spend out of the house."

In my emotionally fragile state, it took all my willpower not to tell her that where I spent my time was Paul's last concern. "Well, actually, I think Paul's worried about me putting on weight," I told her.

"Then just eat less," she stated. And, with that, the discussion was closed.

When I get back to the house with the children, I could hear the shower running and decided not to rush upstairs and ask Paul where he'd been. Later, when the kids were in bed, we'd sit down and have a proper talk. I planned on telling him that I was leaving sometime during the conversation.

At least, that was the plan. Things didn't quite turn out that way.

Chapter Six

HELL

It was after lunch; the kids had eaten and were all sitting on the living room floor watching a movie. Paul had drifted downstairs at some point while I was preparing the meal. He didn't say much before disappearing into his office.

With the children occupied and the house calm and quiet, I decided it was a good time to address the elephant that had been parading around our house for the last few months. It was time to finally confront Paul with what I knew and tell him that I was planning to file for divorce.

I felt my heart beat in my tongue as I nervously approached his office and tapped lightly on the door. Listening, I heard nothing in response. Leaning closer, I knocked at the door again; a little louder this time. Still, I heard no reply and no movement from within the room. Wondering if he'd fallen asleep at his desk or on the small leather couch he kept in there, I gripped the doorknob and slowly twisted it.

"Paul," I quietly called, sticking my head in the gap I'd created.

He wasn't asleep. He was sitting at his desk, leaning far back in his chair and rubbing the fingers of one hand against his jaw. He didn't bother to look up. Instead, his eyes focused on a point in the center of his desktop.

"Paul?" I repeated.

Lifting his gaze, he glowered at me. "I want to talk to you," he stated.

Taking a step inside the room, I nodded. "Actually, I wanted to talk to you too," I added.

"Shut the door," he bluntly ordered.

Curiosity crinkling my eyebrows, I followed his instruction. "So, umm, you spent the whole night out, huh?" I couldn't help but ask as I reached behind me and flicked the door closed with a nudge of my hand.

"Yeah," he nodded unapologetically. "But that's not what I want to talk to you about."

"Oh?" I replied, my brow still knitting in question.

With a sudden lunge, he sat forward and viciously gripped a newspaper that sat folded on the desk.

Tossing it toward me, he barked, "What the hell is this?"

Unaware of what he was talking about, my eyes drifted down to the page. I was looking at the paper upside down, but could see the black and white picture that he was obviously referring to. It was a shot of me and Preston at the charity ball. My memory quickly flashed back to that moment we'd walked off the dance floor, and I mentally kicked myself for not realizing that the photograph could come back to haunt me. Nonetheless, I didn't feel guilty. No, I was still filled with righteous anger. In fact, there was even more of it now. How dare he question me after what he'd been doing?

"Well," he ground out through clenched teeth. "What the hell is that?"

My focus leaving the paper, I met his eyes unflinchingly. "I went to a charity event," I shrugged.

"One you didn't see fit to tell me about?" he shouted, jumping out of his seat. His hand snapped forward and grasped the paper so tightly his knuckles turned white. "One in which you 'the mystery beauty' were on the arm of this...this," he stuttered with anger. "Preston Varrill."

"Verrill," I corrected him. "And it was all perfectly innocent," I added.

"Oh, really?" he scoffed.

"Yes," I insisted. "He wanted a companion to the ball, I went with him."

"Wh...Wh..." he stumbled, shaking his head. "What do you mean, 'he wanted a companion'? What the fuck does that mean? He hired you to do this?" Paul's face was turning a brilliant shade of red and he hadn't appeared to breathe for several seconds.

I refused to answer him. Instead, I kept my eyes on his face, steady and with a calm I had never felt in the face of his anger before.

"This guy paid you to go to this dinner with him?" he demanded, putting the pieces together without any confirmation or denial from me. I wasn't going to lie to him and knew he was intelligent enough to connect the dots alone. "And then what?" he yelled. "What, huh? He fucked you in the back of his limo?"

"No," I replied, my voice and demeanor much more collected than his. "He asked his driver to take me home and he didn't lay a hand on me."

Laughing bitterly, Paul shook his head in disbelief. "You're telling me this guy hasn't screwed you?"

I was tempted to say 'no'. It wouldn't have been a lie. Preston hadn't screwed, banged or fucked me. What we'd shared was something very different. However, I didn't think Paul would appreciate the distinction. In the end, I chose to answer his question with one of my own. Keeping my voice low and carefully measured, I calmly asked, "What right do you have to lecture me? So, it's okay for you to go around sleeping with every woman who crosses your path, but I place a foot wrong and there's hell to pay?"

He blinked and rapidly gave a confused shake of his head. "What are you talking about?"

"I know, Paul," I explained in the same soft, even manner. "I've known for months that you've been having affairs; one night stands with any woman who'll look at you twice, right?" With a self-effacing smile, I forged on. "I was stupid not to have seen it much sooner, but even I'm not blind, Paul. I've seen the emails and that little video; do you masturbate to that often?"

He stared open-mouthed at me, his brain no doubt searching for excuses. However, when he came to the realization that there were none; at least none that any reasonably intelligent person would buy, he went on the offensive. "So, this was your little revenge?" he demanded. "You think I've been unfaithful, so you wanted to get even?" With an angry grunt, he threw the paper back down onto the desk. It skidded off taking a couple of pens and a pad of post-it notes with it.

"No," I responded. "I wanted to get away from you."

"And this guy's your knight in shining armor?" he scornfully asked, as his thick index finger pointed at the newspaper on the floor.

"No," I repeated. "He was a client; a way of making money, so I could support myself."

His eyes seemed to spark with fiery rage and he quickly moved around the desk. I held my ground, refusing to slide back against the wall. In truth, I was terrified, but I wasn't going to give him the pleasure of knowing that he was intimidating me.

Both of his strong hands snatched forward and grasped my upper arms. "You mean he's not the only one?" he spat, roughly jerking me. "What the fuck have you been doing?" he almost screamed, pushing me back until I struck the door. "You've been prostituting yourself to guys like him?" Spittle flew out of his mouth as he screeched and his face was contorted in ugly rage.

I could feel the unpleasantly hot pants of his breath, his face so close to mine. A globule of spit had landed on my cheek and was slowly dribbling down toward my chin. Taking a breath before opening my mouth, I tried to ensure that I wouldn't respond with a knee-jerk statement that would just serve to make him madder. Eventually, I told him, "I've done whatever was necessary."

With a brutal shake of his hands, he banged me against the door harder than before. "And you thought it was necessary to become a whore?" he shouted.

"It's pointless discussing this," I replied, lifting my right hand in an effort to push him away from me. "I'm leaving you, our marriage is over."

"You're fucking right our marriage is over," he confirmed, refusing to slacken his grip on my arms. "And I will make sure my children never see their slut of a mother again."

"Paul," I said, my anxiety growing. I was unable to keep the calm, unaffected tone with which I'd argued with him until that point. "I've done nothing that's harmed the kids; I just needed the money so I could start a life of my own."

"You think the children aren't harmed by having a hooker for a mother?" he bellowed.

"It was never like that," I insisted, wriggling under his grip in attempt to free myself. Suddenly, I felt threatened and trapped, and was fighting to get away from him. Nevertheless, he continued to hold me tightly, refusing to budge. In fact, the more agitated I seemed to get, the more he appeared to enjoy pressing his face close to mine.

"How do I know you haven't been doing this throughout our whole marriage?" he asked. "You blame me; insinuate that I forced you into this, but I don't buy that bullshit. I think you loved it, I think you've always been a cheap, dirty slut."

"Paul, please let go," I mumbled.

At first, my plea caused his fingertips to dig deeper into my flesh. However, with a suddenness that shocked me, he released me. Pushing himself quickly away from me, but still holding out his hands as if they were clinging to something. "I don't know what I was thinking," he whispered, seemingly talking to nobody but himself. "Your disgusting," he added, peering at his hands. "All those men who've had you, all those hands that have been all over you."

"Don't paint yourself out to be some saint in all this," I said, my own anger beginning to creep to the surface. I knew that I shouldn't be irritating him. I knew it would only turn nasty if I pushed his buttons, but still I couldn't manage to keep my mouth shut. "You're not so pure or clean yourself," I insisted.

His eyes lifting from his empty hands, he once more met my face. "Get out of here," he said, quietly but darkly. "Get your stuff and get the fuck out of my house."

"I...I..." I stammered, unsure how to respond or reason with him. "I just need a few days," I urged.

"No," he snapped. "I want you out now."

"Paul," I mumbled, shaking my head incredulous-
ly.

Preempting my thoughts, he didn't wait for me to
voice them. "I don't give a shit where you go. I don't
give a shit what you do. Go and stand on the street
corner and offer blow jobs for a bed. Do whatever the
fuck you want, but you will get the hell out of my
house."

As if my perception of the 'perfect' Paul I'd married had not undergone enough dents, this latest was
incredible. He was a man who claimed to love me; at
one time we were best friends as well as lovers. He
was no more than a stranger to me now. He was a
monster, someone who I quickly realized had hidden
his true nature for years. Then again, maybe not.
Maybe there had been clues I'd chosen to ignore.

"Wh-What about the kids?" I haltingly asked.

"If you think you're taking them with you, think
again," he yelled. "I told you, you're never going to
see them again."

I still wasn't moving, partly out of shock and partly out of a complete inability to know what to do.
Apparently, my lack of action was testing his pa-
tience. With a lunge forward, he whipped his right
hand over his shoulder, before propelling it forward
with a speed and violence that I hadn't time to protect

myself from. The back of his hand struck my cheek with a crack that echoed around the room.

My face instantly stung with a liquid fire that spread across my cheekbone. As I looked up at him with shocked wide eyes, my left hand instinctively lifted to cover the stabbing, as yet invisible, print his hand had left.

Unapologetic and unashamed, Paul was grabbing my shoulder with one hand and the door handle with the other. Pulling me away from the doorway, he yanked it open in fury before gracelessly shoving me across the threshold. "I mean it," he spat. "Get the fuck out and do it now." With that, he slammed the door closed with a bang that reverberated throughout the entire house.

Blinking I realized my eyes were watering; I think it was the sharp sting of my cheek rather than emotional an emotional response that caused the tears, but it would be a lie to say I wasn't also haunted by feelings of grief, anxiety and fear. I was at a loss as to what to do. But I knew two things; if I stayed his violence would escalate and if I even made an attempt to take the kids with me, they would get caught in the brutal middle of it all. For now, at least, I would have to follow Paul's instruction. When I was able to calm down and think clearly, then I could figure out a way to get my children away from him.

I'm not sure why I didn't call the police and have him arrested for hitting me, but in that moment I made the decision not to. Maybe it was to protect the kids from seeing their father hauled away to jail, or maybe it was inner guilt of what I had done.

When the concerned faces of Lizzie and Dylan appeared at the end of the hallway, I tried to force a reassuring smile.

"Is everything okay, Mom?" Lizzie asked.

"Yes, sweetie," I nodded, walking away from Paul's office door and toward the kids.

"We heard banging," she countered.

"And shouting," Dylan chimed in.

"Your dad and I were just having a disagreement," I lied. "It's nothing you need to worry about, okay?"

Both of them looked at me skeptically and I realized they knew I was lying to them. As I reached them, I put one hand around each of their shoulders and steered them back into the living room. "Listen," I began, sighing heavily. "I'm going to have to leave for a while, but I promise I won't be away from you for long."

"What do you mean?" Lizzie asked.

"Why are you going?" Dylan said.

"It's complicated," I muttered, shaking my head. "But I just need you to remember that I'm going to be doing everything I can, and we will work something out." I knew that would mean nothing to them, but I hoped it would stick in their brains nonetheless. Hopefully, if the worst happened, it would make sense one day. At that thought though, I vehemently shook my head. The worst wouldn't come to the worst, because I wasn't going to let anyone take my children from me. If I had to kidnap them, I would.

"Mom?" Lizzie mumbled, peering up at me with concerned eyes.

"Just go back and sit with your little sister," I urged quietly. "I'll explain everything when I can."

Reluctantly both of my older kids obeyed me, settling once more on the rug in front of the TV. I didn't bother to go upstairs and get any clothes. Instead, I kissed each of the children on the top of their heads and told them I would see them soon. It was as though I was just running out to the grocery store except I (and I think they) knew differently.

Chapter Seven

JULIA

Once I left the house and gotten in the car it hit me that I actually didn't have a plan. Looking back, I realize I was in some strange trance-like state and, actually, wasn't doing an awful lot of thinking at all. For instance, I don't remember starting the car. I don't remember backing out of the driveway. I don't remember the road, what turns I took, what traffic lights I passed or even how long I drove for. It's all a messy blur. I didn't know where I was going, but I continued to drive nevertheless.

I suppose I naturally gravitated to the one place I felt safe and the only place I knew Paul wouldn't find me. I vaguely remember sitting in my car in the parking lot opposite Preston's apartment building. I barely recall wondering if I should head up there and if I did, what I would say. I definitely didn't have memories of reaching a decision on that front. But something compelled me to get out of the car and walk across the street.

It was late afternoon when I entered the foyer and Hank was back on duty. I think he spoke to me and I guess I must have responded, because he didn't seem alarmed by my presence. In fact, he didn't even bother to call up to Preston's apartment. Instead, he waved me through, with a comment about the weather.

The next thing I knew I was standing outside Preston's door, sure I should just turn back and walk away. After the way I'd spoken to him, he'd be within his rights to tell me to take a hike. However, he seemed to be the only one I could go to. In retrospect, he wasn't. The truth of the matter is that I went to him because I wanted to go to him. I knew I'd feel comforted simply by his presence. I knew that there were feelings I had when I was around him that I'd never experienced around anyone else; a sense of security that I so desperately needed in those moments.

So, with a nervous finger and a hopeful heart, I reached for the door bell and pushed. The milliseconds dragged on forever as I waited for him to answer. As I did, I ran through a selection of possible openers, 'I'm sorry', 'I made a mistake', 'I shouldn't have snapped at you'. Any and all of those would have been good, but I didn't say any of them. Instead, as the door opened and his slightly confused face began to register mine, I blurted, "Julia."

A mixture of confusion and concern marred his features, as he seemed to discern my haunted expression. "Excuse me?" he mumbled with a half laugh.

"My name," I stated, my voice beginning to get shaky with emotion. Heat swelled in my lower eyelids and an uncomfortable lump in my throat refused to be swallowed. "My name's Julia," I tearfully explained.

He still looked just as confused, but my overflow of emotion caused his concern to rise and he quickly folded an arm around my waist and guided me into the apartment. "Come on," he urged, leading me toward the couch and then suggesting with a slight nudge of his hands that I should sit.

As unbidden tears began to trickle soundlessly down my cheeks, I allowed him to direct my steps and I settled slowly onto the edge of the couch. Once sitting, I leaned my elbows on my knees and dropped my weeping head into my hands.

For a second, Preston stood still, apparently not quite knowing what to do with the emotional wreck that had turned up out of the blue on his doorstep.

However, he quickly shook that off and placed himself on the couch by my side. His jean-clad knee pressed against mine, as he softly asked, "What happened?"

"I behaved awfully toward you," I managed to utter in between sniffs.

He chuckled, before smoothing a hand across my shoulder and rubbing circles between my shoulder blades. "That's not what I meant," he corrected calmly. "I meant what happened since you left here?"

"I didn't know where else to go," I mumbled nonsensically.

Preston must have been confused by the seeming non sequitur, but he didn't fire any further questions at me. Instead, he silently continued to rub the palm of his hand along my back while he waited for me to make sense of what I'd said.

"I...umm....I've made such a mess of everything," I babbled self-pityingly. "I was just trying to get away, that's all I wanted and now I've ruined everything."

"Okay," he said soothingly. "Well, I'm sure we can figure it out. Whatever it is, we can fix it."

I shook my head determinedly. "No, we can't," I told him. "I-"

"Hey," he interrupted, suddenly lifting some of the hair that had fallen across my face. With the backs of his fingers, he gently stroked the spot that Paul had slapped. "What happened to you?" he whispered.

For a moment, I looked at him with alarm, feeling shame, as though what had happened was my fault. To a certain extent, it was my fault, I'd set in motion the chain of events that led to me receiving a backhander to the face. But, of course, I didn't believe there was ever any excuse for violence. That part was solely at the feet of my husband. "I suppose," I breathed, trying to calm my racing heart and brain. "I suppose, I'd better start at the beginning."

Preston didn't look happy with that suggestion; he continued to look with concern at my cheek and wanted an answer to that question first. However, he swallowed that sensation. "Okay," he agreed, nodding. "Start wherever you feel most comfortable."

"I'm married," I stated, a single tear zigzagging down my face and dropping from my trembling chin. "I've been married since I was nineteen. He was my high school sweetheart, and I thought he was the perfect man."

The past tense and the tome I used seemed to leave Preston in no doubt that the man wasn't perfect. He might even have put two and two together and made an assumption about my reddened cheek.

I quickly detailed his background, the wealthy family who thought I wasn't good enough and the prenuptial agreement that I was made to sign. Then, I forged ahead with the next big revelation. "We were happy; at least I thought we were happy. We have three children."

If Preston was shocked or disturbed by that news, he did an excellent job of hiding it. His features remained the same as he intently listened and waited for me to reach the crux of my point.

"Nearly six months ago," I sighed. "I found out Paul was having an affair. Well, that's not quite true; he was having lots of affairs."

His fingers curling over my shoulder, he gave me a squeeze of reassurance while his jaw twitched slightly with the movement of a clenching muscle.

"I wanted to leave, but I couldn't. I had no money, nowhere to go except to a friend who lived halfway across the country, and I knew Paul wouldn't let me leave the state with the kids, so..." I hesitated, suddenly very ashamed to speak the next part of my life history aloud. It was ridiculous really, Preston knew what I was; that's how we'd met. Still, that was before he knew the real me, this was raw and I felt completely exposed. "I had to find a way of making money, preferably a lot of money, and fast."

He nodded his understanding, "So, that's how you got into escorting?" he asked rhetorically.

"Yeah," I replied, in an embarrassed whisper. "I didn't really want to at first, I was scared, but the first couple of times it wasn't too bad, you know?" As I spoke, I kept my eyes on the floor. "And I started to believe that I'd come up with the perfect solution. I was getting my own little revenge and I was making the money I needed to finally leave." Swallowing I shook my head. "And then, one night, I met this guy who was really violent and I realized what I was doing wasn't glamorous or freeing, it was dangerous. So I decided I was going to get out."

"That's what happened to your face?" he asked.

"No, no," I replied. "That was weeks ago now."

"So...?"

"This was my husband," I quickly explained. "The short version is he saw a picture of you and me in the newspaper and he lost his temper."

"Oh, God," he whispered. "I'm so sorry, I should have thought when that guy came up to us-"

"It's not your fault," I quickly interjected. "I should have thought about it, I just didn't stop to consider the consequences."

"Where's your house?" he said sternly, jumping to his feet.

"No," I responded, leaping up and grabbing hold of the waistband of his jeans. "That won't do anything and he's not worth it."

"It'll make me feel better," he countered insistent-
ly.

"Please," I begged. The truth was though, he
wasn't moving. He wasn't trying to force my hand
away from him. He might still have been fighting
with his compulsion to have it out with Paul, but
there wasn't really any chance of him going against
my wishes. "It'll only make things worse," I breathed.

"What do you mean?" he said, shaking his head.
"He can't hurt you now," he added, pulling me into
his arms and wrapping them protectively around my
waist. "You're safe here."

I sniffed into his shoulder and pressed my nose to
his shirt, for a moment just content to breathe him in.
"I know that," I mumbled. "I'm not worried about
myself. I'm worried about my kids."

Tipping his upper body back, so he could look at
my face, he asked, "Are they safe with him?"

"It's not that," I quickly corrected his misunder-
standing. "I know he'd never hurt them."

"But?" he coaxed.

"But he's going to try and take them away from
me. He's going to claim that I'm an unfit mom and
that they're not safe around me."

"Just out of spite?" he asked.

I nodded, finding my hands gripping tightly to
the loose fabric of the back of his shirt. "He's got all of

these lawyers who work for the company and he's got a bunch of friends who are also attorneys, so he won't have a problem fighting me in the courts. I, on the other hand, can now afford to retain a lawyer, but it probably won't leave a lot leftover. And...I'm not sure if I'll be able to win anyway."

"Why do you say that?" Preston whispered, guiding me slowly back down to the couch.

"Because he's rich with powerful friends," I replied as if it were the most obvious answer in the world. "He always wins."

"Maybe not always," he said quietly, seeming to murmur the words more for his own benefit than for mine. "So..." he eventually sighed. "There's something I don't quite understand."

"Go ahead," I sniffed, wiping the heel of my hand across my teary cheek, careful to avoid the soreness just beneath my eye.

"You said you wanted out, that you weren't going to escort after that awful night," he said, but went no further.

"Yeah," I nodded.

"So what changed your mind?" he finally asked. "What made you agree to go out with me?"

With a shaky bottom lip, I opened my mouth to speak and closed it again. Perhaps I'd revealed enough for one afternoon. I'd already burdened the poor man with more than he'd bargained for, he didn't need anything else. "I don't know," I huffed. "I just...You were offering a lot of money and it seemed too good to pass up."

"I'm not sure I believe you," he replied, his eyes unflinchingly fixed on mine. "If it was the money, why didn't you take what I offered this morning?"

"That was..." I babbled. "It was different."

I have no doubt that the answer wasn't satisfactory for Preston. However, he appeared to sense my reluctance to speak further on the subject and duly dropped it. I could see him thinking, I imaginatively thought I could even hear his brain humming, but for a long time he said nothing. When he did speak it was to address his other topic of concern. "Has he ever hurt you before?" he almost whispered. "Your husband?" he added.

"Not really," I numbly responded. "Not like this, not deliberate and..." I paused realizing in my effort to explain, I was making things infinitely muddier than they needed to be. "He's never hit me," I sighed, shaking my head.

"And your kids, did they see it happen?"

"No," I breathed softly. "No, they were in another room."

"How old are they?" he probed. "If you don't mind me asking questions about them," he quickly added.

"It's okay," I smiled sadly, noting that I was actually pleased that he was taking an interest and not just pushing me to the nearest exit. "My eldest, Lizzie, is eight. Dylan is in the middle, he's four and little Kate is turning three in a month."

I suppose he must have seen something in my eyes as I spoke of them, because I certainly didn't say anything particularly revealing. And yet, he observed, "They mean the world to you, don't they?"

Tears seeping onto my cheeks, I tried to sniff them back but couldn't. "Yeah," I blubbed. "I'd do anything for them. And I'm not going to let him take them from me." As words gave way to more full blown weeping, Preston quickly wrapped an arm around me and tugged me close to him. He didn't try to make me stop crying, he simply allowed me to release all of the emotion within me.

"We won't let him," he hummed, rubbing gently circles over the small of my back.

Chapter Eight

LOVE

An hour or so later, once the raw emotions had diluted, I felt embarrassed about the way I'd opened up to him. Preston was undoubtedly a wonderful man, but he was a man I'd known for less than two weeks. No matter how strong the attraction between us, he can't have been ready for the wealth of confessing I'd just done.

But nothing was said for some time. We simply sat in mutual silence.

However, what began as a comfortable silence soon became awkward. What was he thinking? Did he wonder what the hell he'd gotten himself into? Did he wish he had never contacted me? The less emotionally charged I grew, the more self-conscious and anxious I became about what was roaming around in his mind.

Eventually, the desperation to know what he was thinking became too great. "I'm sorry I dumped this all on you," I mumbled quietly.

"Don't apologize," he urged, shaking his head which was rested in the corner of the couch. "I'm glad that you told me."

"Really?" I asked, lifting my cheek from his shoulder, so I could look squarely into his face. "Little too much, don't you think?" I added, trying to lighten the moment with a smile that didn't reach the rest of my face let alone my eyes.

"Well," he conceded warmly. "I didn't quite expect that," he admitted quietly. "But I knew you had to be in some kind of trouble, and I really am pleased you felt comfortable enough to speak to me."

I offered him a shy, grateful and slightly more genuine smile. "I don't really know why that is..." I mumbled. "Why I feel comfortable talking to you," I added.

"I don't think the 'why' really matters," he insisted gently. "All that matters is that you did, and I want to help you."

Shaking my head, the smile dropped from my face. "Look," I sighed. "I appreciate it, really I do, but money isn't going to solve the problem."

"I'm not talking about money," he replied, sitting forward and adjusting the glasses at the bridge of his nose. "I'm talking about legally."

"Legally?"

"If your husband is serious about trying to take your children from you, I can help."

I observed him for a moment, trying to assess whether he was serious. "You could do that?" I asked.

Grinning, he nodded. "I think so," he assured me.

"But?" I babbled uselessly.

"I'm a corporate lawyer at the moment," he admitted, his eyes moving toward his feet. "But before that, I practiced family law. So, I know a thing or two about child custody battles."

Unsure what to say, I simply stared dumbfounded at him. His eyes were sincere, it was not an empty offer of help, he intended to follow through.

"Your husband hasn't got a leg to stand on," he quickly continued, perhaps misinterpreting my silence as concern over the case. "He can't prove you've done nothing illegal and you've certainly done nothing that has affected the safety or happiness of your kids. If he tries to suggest you're an unfit mother, he's going to look like a fool."

"But," I uneasily said, shuffling in the seat. "Paul's got an army of powerful attorneys, they'll pin something on me."

"Surely, the only thing they can prove is that you've offered your services as an escort; a date for dinners, a friendly ear over a few drinks. There's nothing illegal or immoral about that."

"What if they find one of my clients?" I whispered. "What if they find someone who'll testify to what I've done?"

"I don't think any of your clients are going to want to be found," he immediately assured me, shaking his head. "And no matter how much money your husband's lawyers offer them, they sure as hell won't want to publicly announce that they've paid for sex. They would be admitting to a criminal act."

I wasn't completely reassured, but I nodded slightly. He had a point. Many of my clients were married or in relationships; all of them, except Chris, had jobs - well-paying ones at that; they had reputations to consider, and had a lot to lose by admitting to our 'business' arrangements.

Preston nudged me from my contemplative silence, by resting his hand reassuringly on my knee. "It's going to be okay," he reminded me. "No matter what he throws at us, he won't win."

A grateful half smile did nothing to hide my doubt and I felt compelled to explain it. "He'll fight dirty if he has to," I softly said.

With a self-effacing tilt of his head, he grinned. "I can fight dirty if the need arises," he muttered. Then, his features tightened and he looked at me with grave seriousness. "I won't let him take your kids from you, Julia."

Another lump was rising in my throat and I felt my bottom lip tremble. I bit down hard on it, both to stop the shaking and prevent a further flood of uncontrollable tears.

"Julia," he repeated quietly. "Julia," he said again, as if he was trying the name out for size in his mouth. His lips began to curve. "Julia," he mumbled a third time, breaking into a grin. "Yeah," he eventually sighed. "I think that works."

I puffed out a breath of amusement, but couldn't quite bring myself to share his broad smile. "Why?"

"Umm, because it fits," he chuckled. "It's you."

"No, that's not what I meant," I rapidly corrected him. "I mean, why do you want to help me? Why would you go through all of this trouble? I'm a stranger to you."

"Are you?" he asked, his chocolaty eyes focusing intently on mine.

Trying to swallow, my head moved in an indefinite dance of nods, shakes and shrugs.

"I know we haven't known each other very long," he added calmly. "I know it might seem insane, and believe me it's not something I expected. I just wanted some company at that ball, but I didn't... I didn't bargain for what happened when I met you."

I was almost scared to ask, but he remained silent, waiting for me to speak before he'd explain. My words came numbly, my mouth moving of its own volition and the breath coming shakily. "What happened?"

He smiled a little and then cocked his head to one side. "Do you really have to ask?" he countered.

"Well," I wavered, stopping when tears threatened to spill over once more. Sniffing, I tried to compose myself, but was so acutely aware of the tightness in my throat that it was impossible to focus on anything else. "I know how I feel. I don't really understand it," I managed to whisper. "But I..." Eventually, I gave up the attempt to speak.

"I've fallen in love with you," he whispered, his fingers moving tenderly over my shoulder. Then, gradually he dipped his head toward mine, his gorgeous, soft, wonderful lips drawing ever closer.

I'd thought I wanted him to say those words; believed that it would help make sense of my own strong emotions. Instead, it just scared me. He didn't know what he was doing; what he was getting himself into. Once he had a chance to really think about it, he'd realize how insane it all was. He'd want a woman who *hadn't* sold herself to strangers. As much as I wanted to believe I hadn't changed, that I was still the pure unsullied Julia, it simply wasn't true. I was tainted by what I'd done. Maybe Paul was right, the children shouldn't be around me. But I certainly knew that I didn't deserve to be loved by a good man; the best I'd ever met.

As his mouth met mine, I froze, passively accepting his kiss, but doing nothing in return. It prompted him to quickly pull away. "What's wrong?" he asked.

"I...umm...think I'd better go," I breathed.

His face continued to hover close to my own. "Go where?" he quietly asked, remembering that I'd said I had nowhere else to go.

"Hotel," I shrugged.

"You don't have to," he replied, his left hand brushing the strands of hair that were curtaining my face behind my ear. "I'd like you to stay," he added.

"I don't think that's a good idea," I responded, avoiding his eyes.

Gently, taking my chin in his thumb and finger, he forced me to look at him. "I know you're scared," he began solemnly. "You don't know me that well, and you have no reason to believe that you can trust me."

"I do trust you," I interjected quickly. "I don't know why, but I always have."

A thin smile graced his lips before he continued. "Then, what are you scared of?" he asked.

"I...I..." I fumbled, sucking in labored breaths as I tried to put my thoughts into words and comprehensible sentences. "I'm scared of the way I feel," I sighed. "The power of it, the fact that I have no control. Ever since I met you, I've been doing and saying things that a part of me knew I shouldn't." I barely paused for breath, before rambling onward. "But I was incapable of stopping myself. And the thing that scares me the most is that, at some point, you're going to come to your senses and realize what a mistake this all is."

"Woah, woah," he mumbled. "What are you talking about?"

"Oh, come on, Preston," I muttered, shaking my head wearily. "Are you really going to want to be with me after everything I've done? You really want to love a whore?"

"I told you," he quickly replied, "You're not a whore."

"You may not choose to use that word," I argued. "But that's exactly what I was." After a beat of silence, I corrected myself. "That's what I am."

He was silent for what felt like an eternity. Neither of his hands moved and his face remained close to mine. He was thinking, trying to find the right words; because, I suppose, he thought his response was crucial. And he was right. But, fortunately for both him and I, he was a master at treading carefully. "Look," he began, swallowing before fixing his eyes on mine and keeping them there throughout the next few moments. "I'm not going to pretend that I'm thrilled about what you had to do, but I know that you were desperate and you thought you were out of options." He calmly moistened his lips and forged on. "I don't blame you for the decisions you made, Julia," he insisted. "I don't think any less of you for them and I don't think they make you unworthy of being loved." Tenderly, he stroked the curve of my chin with his thumb. "I didn't fall in love with you because of what you were doing. I didn't fall in love with you in spite of it, either. I just love you, and I know that I would regardless of how we met."

I wanted to ask him how he managed it; how he found the perfect words and the sincerity to say them with. If anything, his little speech made me feel even less deserving of him. However, rather than exacer-

Clara James

bating the fear of his sudden change of heart, I was filled with a desire to prove that I would return that unconditional love. I would do everything in my power to be the woman he deserved.

"Are you okay?" he whispered, noting my quiet contemplating.

"I..." I breathlessly attempted to speak. "I don't know how I got so lucky," I softly explained. "But I do know that I'm not going to make any more stupid mistakes that I would end up regretting for the rest of my life."

Preston looked worried, his eyebrows knitting together.

Quickly, I opened my mouth again. "I'm not going to let my childish fears push you away," I added. "I love you," I said, fighting giggles of relief. The sound of those words felt good in my mouth, they sounded good in my ears. So good, they needed repeating. "I love you," I grinned, feeling freer and more alive than I had in months, maybe even years.

His cute lopsided smile lit his face and created a sparkle in both eyes. "Then I think we can work through everything else," he reasoned, his lips still distorted in joy.

Overwhelmed by affection for him, I grasped the front of his shirt in my right hand and tugged his face down to mine. I attacked his mouth with a passion, longing and tenderness that I'd felt unable to fully express before. There were no secrets between us anymore. He knew everything and it hadn't made him run the other way. He knew the real me, I could now be the real me. I no longer had to pretend to be unaffected by his presence, I no longer had to fight it or remind myself that it would only end badly. In that instant, I had no idea how things would ultimately end, but I wasn't going to let the possibility of happiness pass me by.

With a chuckle of surprise and a groan of delight, Preston quickly returned my kiss with fervor and soulful affection.

For a long time, we both simply reveled in that joining of lips. It was fiery at times, full of enthusiasm and need, but it wasn't an overture for something more. We were enjoying that kiss for the pleasure it offered in and of itself, and it was all the more satisfying for that. It was a kiss of forgiveness, a kiss of promise and a kiss that seemed to mark a fresh start. For me, at least, that was certainly the case. For me, it was a kiss of offering. I was giving myself to him. Not just my body this time, something far more precious.

Chapter Nine

GOOD MORNING

That kiss never really developed into anything more. I'd expected it to, perhaps we both did. However, upon reflection, that night seems more perfect because we didn't make love. I think we were both exhausted, emotionally at least, and Preston had taken on his gentlemanly mantel once more. He made it very clear, through his actions rather than words, that he would not rush anything. In fact, when our mouths finally parted, he offered me his spare bedroom.

"I don't want to be alone," I answered.

With an understanding smile and a nod, he reached down for my hand, gently coaxed me to my feet and led me to his room. From a drawer he grasped a T-shirt and handed it to me. Then, he wandered to a door in the corner of the room that opened into his large en suite bathroom. "I think there is a new toothbrush in the cabinet," he said, pointing to a wall-mounted cabinet above the sink. "You're welcome to it."

I brushed my teeth, washed my streaky face, stripped off and put on the T-shirt. I held it to my face as I pulled it over my head. It smelled so reassuringly of him. Even though it was freshly cleaned, his scent lingered on the shirt and it was heavenly.

Eventually, I walked barefoot back into the bedroom and found he'd already readied himself for bed. He was dressed in boxers and also had a T-shirt on. Asking if I was okay, he yanked down the sheets and gestured for me to choose a side.

I didn't mind, and simply shrugged, before selecting the side I'd slept on the night before. Preston then turned out the lights and got into bed next to me. He immediately shuffled close placing his arms around me and pulling me to his chest. I automatically draped a hand around his waist, but found the feel of cotton unsatisfactory and sought for the warm, solid flesh I knew was beneath.

Instinctively, Preston sensed my frustration and released me long enough to sit up and chuck his shirt over his head. Once he was laid down again, I placed the palm of my hand in the center of his naked chest and gave a contented mewl. However, after a few moments, I still felt that something wasn't quite right. Soon, I was sitting up and pulling my own shirt off.

Completely naked, I settled back onto the mattress and pressed myself to him. Flesh against flesh, except for his boxers. Strangely, there was almost nothing sexual about our intimate position. Neither of us were turned on, we just found comfort in the closeness, scent and warmth of each other's body. Preston began to fidget, feeling perhaps overdressed, he nudged his boxers off his hips and then kicked them down and toward the bottom of the bed. When he pulled me close again, it was with a sigh of fulfillment. Both arms tightly wrapped around his waist, I slipped one leg between his strong, muscular ones. His flaccid manhood was pressed securely along my thigh, my mound solidly pushed against his hip. We were as one. Not in the literal sense perhaps, but, in that moment, I was more connected with him than I had ever been with any man in my life.

Listening to the soft, reassuring thud of his heartbeat and luxuriating in his warmth, which surrounded me like the warm rays of spring sunshine, I slipped into a wonderfully comforting and cleansing sleep.

Clara James

Several hours later, I awoke to find the bed next to me empty and whimpered grumpily at the loss. Forcing my eyes open, I lifted me head fractionally from the pillow and listened to the soft stream of a shower. It wasn't coming from the en suite, it was further down the hall and I guessed he'd deliberately left the closest bathroom free for me. Rolling over and finding the bed suddenly much too large to be alone in, I glanced at the clock. It was a little after eight in the morning.

Feeling tired, but desperately lonely in the large bed, I heaved myself up and out from beneath the covers. I made my way to the bathroom, relieved my bladder and then brushed my teeth. As I gazed at my sleepy reflection, I noticed that the mark of Paul's hand was beginning to show more prominently. My eyes lingered there for a moment, but my brain was zoned out. It was as if it didn't matter any more. It happened; it was unpleasant, but it was over. And it really was over, I knew that for certain.

I didn't bother to cover my nakedness before pulling the shower cubicle door and stepping in. At first, the spears of water were freezing and I yelped, trying to dodge out of their way. However, they quickly rose to a comfortable temperature and I surrendered myself to its purifying power. I don't think I'd been in long before I heard a soft creak of the door.

The Escort Next Door III

Through the frosted glass of the door, I saw a blurry Preston, bare-chested with a towel draped around his waist. "Sorry," I heard him say over the noise of the shower. "Just want to brush my teeth."

"It's fine," I called back. But as I watched the taut muscles of his back while he moved in front of the sink, 'fine' was not the word I would have used to describe my emotions. Feeling mischievous and with a childlike grin on my face I grabbed the edge of the shower door and slid it open a few inches. A fine mist of water was escaping though the gap as I leaned my face out of it. "Hey," I smiled, watching what I could see of his face in the fogged mirror. He was wearing his glasses and had the toothbrush in his mouth, with foamy toothpaste creeping out of the corners. "You want to come in here?" I suggested.

"Hmm," he hummed, his mouth still full of bubbly paste. With a quick spit in the sink, he looked up in the mirror and found my face in the reflection. "I've already taken a shower in the other room, thanks," he smiled, giving me a grateful nod before resuming his vigorous brushing.

"I know," I informed him with a giggle. "But do you want to come in here?" I repeated a little more saucily than before.

His eyebrows rose and his hand stilled. "Oh," he said, the word muffled around the toothbrush. Slowly, he slipped it from his mouth and he began to smile. "Oh," he repeated.

"So, you getting in or not?" I asked, laughing at his hesitancy. Curling my right leg around the shower door I rubbed the arch of my foot up and down the edge, hoping that it looked sexy.

His smile grew broader, as he placed the toothbrush on the edge of the sink. "Give me one second," he said. I lost sight of his face, as he quickly bent at the waist and drew in large mouthfuls of water from the faucet. He quickly swilled and spat, then slipped his spectacles off his nose and tossed them down on the counter. Then, he whirled around and with one hand pulled the towel from his waist. "I was going to ask how you're feeling this morning," he chuckled, gripping the door and sliding it wide open. He didn't seem to care about the needles of water that started a small puddle on his floor. "I guess, I've got my answer," he added with playful waggle of his eyebrows.

As he quickly tugged the shower door closed and his face finally got a good look of mine, his features darkened. For a second, I didn't realize what was troubling him, but as he reached forward with his left hand and cupped my cheek, I made the connection.

"It's okay," I told him softly, flashing him a reassuring smile.

"No it's not," he insisted. "It's far from okay."

The Escort Next Door III

With the jets of water striking the top of my neck and rolling down my back, I slid my wet fingers over his and clasped his hand. I lifted it slightly from my face, just far enough for me to turn my mouth toward his palm and tenderly press my lips to it. "It is okay," I reiterated. "It doesn't matter any more." Easing my free hand around the back of his neck, I tugged his face down and delicately molded my mouth to his. It was a brief kiss of reassurance and as I tipped my head back, I smiled at him. "This is all that matters now."

A little reluctantly, he nodded. "Yeah," he agreed.

"Come here," I urged, stepping back until I was fully under the water and taking him with me. The stream struck him just beneath the chin and beaded down his chest in sexy rivulets that mesmerized me. His torso was the most beautiful thing I'd seen, to view water droplets caress that skin, making it even sleeker and shiny, was another revelation.

As the path of water moved to his hips and thighs, my gaze became focused on his shaft, which was hanging unresponsively between his legs. My knee-jerk reaction was to feel offended. I was naked, and I thought he'd understood that I wasn't inviting him into the shower to help wash my back. Surely, all men got immediately hard in that situation. However, when my attention snapped back to his face, I saw him still examining my cheek with a concerned look worming its way deeper and deeper into his brow.

"Preston," I whispered, trying to coax his focus to my eyes, although I would have accepted any other part of my body too.

"Hmm?" he mumbled, slowly lifting his serious gaze a couple of inches.

Moving the hand that I continued to hold, I guided his palm to my abdomen. Pressing him to my belly, I ushered his fingers in small circles over my glistening, smooth skin. My other hand slipped from his neck, over the front of his shoulder and traced one firm pec. Then I followed the line of his sternum and the valley between his abs. Reaching his belly button, I let the tip of my finger dance around the edge, before moving down to his pubic bone and the neat patch of hair that covered it.

No longer needing me to coax his hand, Preston's fingers drifted upward. He caressed the curve of one breast, taking the weight in his palm and gently teasing my nipple with his fingertips.

By the time my fingers reached his shaft, he was already hardening. When I wrapped my hand around him and gently stroked up and down, he grew exponentially. It was a sudden burst of arousal that made him rigid and ready. The velvety soft skin of his manhood seemed to coat solid steel. The feeling of his firmness caused a swell of desire in me.

The hand at my breast had gone still; he continued to hold me but was no longer massaging my tender skin. When I looked up into his face, I found his eyes closed in concentration, his tongue flicking over his bottom lip.

"I want you," I whispered, taking a shuffled, sliding step back until I met the cold wall.

His eyelids quivered open and he stepped toward me, squashing his hand between our upper bodies and my hand between our lower. When his hip met mine, I lifted my left leg, rubbing my inner thigh against his outer, before lifting my knee all the way to his waist.

Preston's breath was coming hard as he leaned forward, his panting mouth so close to mine. With winded half-gasps, he tried to kiss me, clasping at my lips in a wet, desperate, shaky grappling that nibbled at me and gave me brief tastes of his minty tongue.

The shower water was washing over our faces, entering our opened mouths as we both began to gulp in air as quickly as we could. The fingers that I held tightly on his member were between my thighs, the head of his shaft pressing against my folds. I guided him down just an inch until he was perfectly aligned with my passage. Then, I released my grip on him and snaked my arm around his shoulder.

I felt his chest heaving violently against mine, setting my nipples on fire with the sensual play of his chiseled physique. His hips were edging forward, but he was doing so agonizingly slowly. No thrusting occurred at that stage, no dips in and out to gently prepare my body. Instead, he warmed me up with a long, smooth entrance that gradually extended my sex.

It was sweet torture, wanting so desperately to be filled, but feeling every slight twitch and movement he made as he dragged out the pleasure of our joining. My eyes slipped shut, my head tipped back against the tiled wall and I drew in urgent lungful's of air. My hands were entwined at the back of his neck and I pulled him fiercely to me, my lips moving soundlessly and brushing over the freshly shaved skin of his cheek.

His thick rigidness finally reached its hilt and he was enclosed tightly within my clenching and quivering sex. "Julia," he said softly, uttering my name as if it were a secret only we shared; as if it were something precious. "Oh, Julia," he repeated, groaning this time in pleasure, his hips grinding against mine.

That sound, the sound of *my* name spoken in gratification and thrill, in his deep, tender voice was by the far the most erotic moment of my life at that point. And I climaxed, right then and there; I squirmed at the sudden onset of swirling warmth and uncontrollable spasms. "Oh, God," I panted. "Preston," I mumbled.

His body wasn't quite motionless, but he wasn't thrusting. Instead, he gently moved his hips, circling them soothingly and teasing his pubic bone against my clitoris.

"Ahhh," I screeched. "Say it again!" Among the cries, my hands were tangling into his wet hair, trying desperately to grasp him.

"Julia," he whispered intimately into my ear.

Another convulsion of pleasure rocked through me and I bucked against his hips.

He was still breathing hard, I could feel and hear that. And yet, he was somehow finding the presence of mind to control himself. He continued to do so until the orgasm that was causing my entire body to shake subsided. With a genuine smile, he looked into my barely focused eyes. "You okay?" he asked.

I nodded as best I could with a neck that felt like Jello.

His grin growing wider, he began to move. It was slow at first, while he coaxed my body back into the game. A rhythmic writhing that called primordially to my entire being: body, mind and soul. The movement was occupied by his masculine, breathy grunts, a sound that was almost as magical to my ears as the sound of him whispering my name. Soon, he felt me respond; my hands gripping him tightly, my sex completely open to him, my lips caressing his face and neck as I murmured sounds and words that I hoped would spur him on.

Preston then began to move with purpose, our wet bodies meeting smoothly each time, melding to each other as though we were actually moving as one. We were in sync, there was no rough bumping of hips, no harsh slap of skin on skin. Instead, we withdrew and thrust in perfect harmony. Our bodies constantly sought the other out, see-sawing in a desperate attempt not to let go.

It was bliss, perfection; it was so much more than just sex. And it felt incredible. He was me, I was him; we were both taking and giving pleasure in equal measure. And this time, when I crested the height of ecstasy, he was right there with me. While I whimpered his name and my body clamped aggressively around his manhood, his body was convulsing and offering me its warmth.

"I..." he breathed, his hips jerking. "I love you," he grunted, with one final lazy thrust.

White spots dancing in front of my closed eyelids and blood pulsing hard against my eardrums, I slowly stroked the back of his neck, silently willing him not to pull away too soon. He didn't seem to have any intention of moving though. His cheek was pressed to mine, his forehead, resting on the wall next to my head.

"I love you," I replied, my voice sounding very distant.

Chapter Ten

ESCAPE

An hour later; it felt like those wonderful moments in the shower were just a dream. We were sitting in his living room, me cross-legged on the couch wearing the jeans I'd been wearing the night before and one of his sweaters, while he was perched on the edge of his coffee table with his open laptop resting on his legs.

It was stupid of me to suppose that reality couldn't disturb us, but I'd hoped that, even just for that one day, we could pretend there was no one else in the world. Preston, however, had gone into 'mission' mode.

"I think it would help if you file for divorce first," he said. "And cite his infidelity as the reason."

"I can't prove that though, he's bound to have deleted all of that stuff from his computer by now."

"It doesn't matter," he dismissed with a flick of his hand before adjusting his glasses.

"Well," I mumbled doubtfully. "It'll seem strange that I didn't leave him right away, won't it?"

"No," he insisted. "The prenup put you in an impossible position."

I nodded and listened to him plan the case he would put forward. He had obviously been thinking about it and I wondered if he'd lain awake the night before formulating his plan of attack. He was prepared for things to get messy; prepared for his relationship with me to be called into question, but he didn't seem fazed by any of it. In fact, he seemed to be excited by it. I would later find out that his enthusiasm was a desire to teach my husband a lesson. I'm sure Preston doesn't have a violent bone in his body, but he wanted to punish Paul and intended to hit him where it hurt the most.

The more he talked about the possible fallout, the angle Paul's lawyers would take, and how they'd try to discredit me, the more alarmed I became. This was all incredibly frightening to me and I asked him on more than one occasion whether it was really something he wanted to insert himself in the middle of.

But he brushed my concern aside with a smile and an assurance that we were in it together, no matter what.

As it turned out, Paul had been in the midst of filing for divorce too, and despite my belief that he wouldn't find me at Preston's house, later that evening, a messenger arrived and served me with papers.

The case dragged on for weeks, and then months. During that time, I only saw my children on brief visits, which were all conducted at the home of Paul's parents. Both of them had heard Paul's side of the story and only just managed to be civil to me in front of the kids. Out of earshot, they didn't hold back.

Over the course of the legal battle, I wasn't eating or sleeping properly; I lost weight and spent much of the time in a depressive funk. Preston was there through it all, handling my moods, constantly reassuring me and never giving up. However, he never really told me what he'd been hanging our case on.

And then one day, around mid March, he pulled an ace out of his sleeve: Lyra.

The girl was only nineteen, had beautiful long blonde hair, a perfect round face, slender figure and ample curves. She was an attractive girl, of that there was no doubt. When she turned up at the family court, she was wearing a charcoal skirt suit with a pink blouse. Despite all her beauty and obvious attributes, Lyra looked haunted, almost as depressed as

I was at that time. In the silence of the court, I peered questioningly at Preston before noticing the murmurs of concern from Paul's table of lawyers.

"Thanks for coming, Ms. Raines," Preston said, lifting himself from his seat. "I'd just like to ask you a few questions, if I may?"

She nodded, her eyes drawn to Paul.

"I know this isn't easy for you," Preston added. "But, what is or was the nature of your relationship with Mr. Hayes?"

"I..." she began shakily before clearing her throat. "I'm his personal assistant," she sighed. "And...umm...we were having an affair."

"A sexual relationship?" Preston asked, seeking clarification for the benefit of the judge.

"Yes," she confirmed with a nod.

"And when did that start?" he continued.

"Umm," she hesitated. "It was...err..." she looked around nervously.

"It's okay," Preston softly soothed. "Just tell the truth."

"It was over two years ago," she quickly admitted.

The rumble of conversation got louder in Paul's camp, while my jaw dropped open. Not only had Paul been unfaithful for much longer than I'd realized, he'd made the stupid, unforgivable decision to have sex with an underage girl.

"How old were you at that time?" Preston asked, again seeking clarification of something the rest of us had already figured out on our own.

"Seventeen," she mumbled.

"Objection, your honor," the head of Paul's team. "This isn't relevant to the activities of Mrs. Hayes."

Preston spun on the arch of his foot to face the overzealous lawyer. "It has everything to do with Mrs. Hayes," he insisted. "Because it proves the extent of deception that Mr. Hayes is capable of and, more importantly, the possible sex crimes he has committed.

Banging a gavel, the judge called silence. "I'll allow it," the older gentleman sighed. "Continue, Mr. Verrill."

What followed was Lyra's description of how she'd been seduced by Paul's success and money and flattered by the attention he lavished on her. Filling in the blanks in her story, I assumed Paul realized he'd made a catastrophic error in judgment when he slept with her the first time. And in order to keep her quiet, he'd continued to see her; even got her a job in the company all just to keep her happy. But she'd thought she was the only one. When the rumors started flying around the office, she confronted him and he tried to buy her silence.

It seems she wanted revenge more than she wanted money.

Sure enough, she got it. That afternoon, Paul's attempt to claim sole custody of the children was thrown out. I was awarded principle custody, and he was given limited visitation rights.

Sadly, no criminal case was brought against Paul for his relationship with Lyra, because she refused to testify against him. When Preston and I spoke to her outside the court house, she said she'd been foolish to believe him, but he didn't force her into anything and she could not in good conscience claim that he had.

I admired her for that.

"Besides," she shrugged. "After this hits the newsstands, I don't think Paul Hayes is going to find it very easy to enjoy the kind of life he's become accustomed to."

She was right, the company would undoubtedly lose clients, Paul would certainly lose friends, and there would be many women who would avoid him at all costs.

Preston and I watched Lyra walk away. We were side by side, our arms brushing against each other, and we remained silent until she'd disappeared into a crowd of people.

"How did you know about her?" I asked, breaking the companionable silence and spinning my face to his.

"Did a little digging," he responded mysteriously. "You told me Paul and his cronies would play dirty, I knew I'd have to play dirty, too," he added. "And I had a hunch that there would be a scorned woman somewhere in your husband's past. You can't go around treating people that way and not make some enemies."

"True," I acknowledged, feeling foolish that I hadn't been the one to suggest we find an angry lover.

"I'm sorry that I've been difficult these last few weeks," I whispered sincerely.

"It's okay," he said, shaking his head. "You were going through a lot and you were frightened, it's understandable."

"But it's all over now, right?" I asked, a little wary when asking him to confirm my hope.

He removed his hand from his pocket and held it open toward me. "It's all over," he said. "You can go and pick your children up first thing tomorrow and we can move on."

Hesitantly, I reached forward, slipping my fingers through his. "Are you ready for that?" I asked. "I mean, suddenly being in a relationship with a woman who has three children."

Preston made an uncomfortable face. "You think they'll like me?"

Letting out a breath of laughter, I squeezed his hand. "I think they'll love you, the question is how will you cope? Are you really ready for all of this? Do you want to be involved in raising another man's children?"

Turning his head slightly, he tugged on my hand and we both began to walk up the street. "Listen," he said, as soon as we were moving. "I'm sure it's going to be a steep learning curve and I'm certain that I'm going to get some things wrong," he added with a chuckle. "But I love you," he stated simply, as though that one simple statement answered any further questions. "These kids are a part of you, how can I not love them too?"

"You know," I mumbled, peering up into his soft face and wondering how anyone who looked so meek and unassuming could be such a pit bull in the courtroom. "You are one smooth talker, Preston Verrill."

That night, back at his apartment, he'd arranged a celebratory dinner with three courses and a bottle of expensive champagne. All of which went un-eaten and un-drunk. As soon as we got through the door, I couldn't resist the urge to pull him to me and kiss him with a pent up passion and frustration of several weeks. Things escalated quickly from there and we ended up making love on his hardwood floor, with a desperation and need that I don't think either of us had felt before.

It was a need to get back to that morning in the shower; to remind ourselves of the way that wonderful freedom had felt. Only it was even better, because this time we truly were free. There was nothing hanging over us anymore. Everything really was going to be all right.

The rendezvous on the floor was quick and, for us at least, a lot less graceless than we'd become use to. It offered both of us a much needed release of heated lust, but it was nowhere near enough. We spent the next three hours showing each other, in a variety of ways, just how in love we were. Eventually, it was exhaustion rather than a complete lack of desire that prompted us to collapse breathlessly onto the bed.

I was atop him, my legs straddling his hips, my cheek pressed to his chest and our sweaty bodies still fighting for oxygen. His molten liquid was warming my core, which flexed with the aftershocks of the most recent explosive orgasm.

Eventually, I lifted my head and brushed the hair away from my face. Staring down into his peaceful features, which were so close to sleep, I bent to kiss the tip of his sweaty nose. "Thank you," I quietly said.

"What for?" he countered, not bothering to open his weary eyes.

"For everything," I sighed, my hands resting on his shoulders, as I staunchly refused to disconnect our lower halves. "For seeing the best in me," I began. "For not letting me push you away, for getting my children back, for loving me..." I trailed off, realizing the list could go on all night. However, I quickly decided there was an umbrella thank you. "For being you," I said, tipping forward, so I could lay on him once more. This time, I placed my face on the pillow next to his, turning so my lips were a breath from his cheek.

"Actually," he mumbled, forcing his eyes open and turning his face to mine. Our noses collided causing us both to giggle before he continued. "There's something I want to ask you," he whispered in the darkness.

"You can ask me anything," I replied, with a deliriously happy chuckle.

"Well, you know," he began, not quite sharing my high and gazing at me with serious eyes. "I've been doing a lot of thinking lately."

"Hmm," I responded urging him to continue.

"You know, during the court proceedings one of the things I hated most was having to call you Mrs. Hayes."

"Umm, ok" I mumbled ineffectually.

"Well, you won't have to call me anything but 'Julia' ever again."

"Yeah," he smiled. "But I was wondering if you'd thought about changing your last name?"

Blinking, I peered curiously at him for a moment, thinking it was an odd time to bring this conversion up. Nevertheless, I was happy to respond. "Going back to my maiden name? I suppose I will, but-"

"No," he quickly interjected, silencing me with his index finger against my lips. "That's not exactly what I had in mind."

With his finger still pressed to my mouth, I wasn't able to reply verbally, but I gave him a perplexed shrug of one shoulder.

"I was thinking..." he stopped, shook his head and muttered something beneath his breath. "I'm doing this all wrong," he said. "But I was wondering if you'd thought about changing your name to Mrs. Verrill?"

"Huh?" I muttered, his fingertip still blocking any effort to speak.

"Julia," he continued, slowly slipping his hand away from my mouth and caressing my cheek. "Will you marry me?"

"I...I..." I babbled, between giggles. "Are you serious?" I blurted. "Yes, yes, yes," I excitedly squealed, punctuating each word with a kiss to his eyelids and cheeks. "Of course, I'll marry you."

After answering that fateful question, I knew that my children and I would live, in our own way, happily ever after.

~THE END~

Thanks for reading!!

Also by bestselling author

Clara James

~The Escort Next Door Series~

The Escort Next Door

The Escort Next Door: Captivated

The Escort Next Door: Escape

~Her Last Love Affair Series~

Her Last Love Affair

Her Last Love Affair: Breathing Without You

Her Last Love Affair: The Final Journey

To view these titles visit:
http://amzn.to/15ek5q7

29218836R00076

Printed in Great Britain
by Amazon